Always Watching

By Dan J. Pease

Table of Contents

Dedications

Dedicated to my parents, my Nannie Sallie, my uncle David, and Emlyn Moment, all have inspired me for great aspirations.

Preface

We have all heard the stories of ghosts, demons, and ghouls that have filled our heads and our hearts with fear and dread. Stories that have been a highlight of Halloween: The October occasion honoured by the terrifying, one of the most exciting and dark times of the year for those who have the stomach for it.

But, in all the years of the childish traditions, there is always one such story unnatural for the ear, one so haunting, if any child as to be told, by accident or otherwise, they would succumb to poisoned nightmares and scream out in the dead of night.

A story that must be seen to be believed.

This story took place at a time where members of staff found it hard to control even their own lives, let alone their students. Life was hard for everyone, regardless of what background they came from. Many had families to go home to at night. Many were forced to fend for themselves and live the feelings of being looked down on and abandoned in the cold.

Who listens to you when you are alone?

Where is that shoulder to cry on if you are in the dark?

Why are we made to talk to ourselves all the time because no one will care to listen to our pleas?

Just bear it in mind that you are never on your own. 'Just remember, wherever you are in the world, someone is always watching you and what you do.'

The Heat

Our story began on a hot day in May. Term 5 at an old high school was about to come to an end. The boiling hot sun was beating down on the school's inhabitants with immeasurable heat. The temperature was as high and as overwhelming as ever. It was nothing like any summer the school had lived through before.

The schoolyard looked like a wasteland for anyone who came to see it. It smelt like one too, with all the dirty wrappers lying all over the floor. The green grass was a mustard shade. It resembled that same condiment that was sold in the school canteen. For the staff who worked in it, that was one of the hottest places on the entire grounds. Other boiling places included several of the classrooms, the bathrooms around the school gym, and the library. The grass was dying as well from the over-bearing heat. Even blowing it over with the breath from the lungs would kill it instantly. And just as it floated through the air, it would disintegrate like wood on a fireplace.

The playground was a mess too. The climbing frames were as rusty as an engine sold for scrap, ready to be broken up and melted down for parts. Even on a good day, the climbing frames were not safe to play on in their condition. The tarmac the climbing frames sat in had become weak. By standing on it, it felt like it was melting. This would make it as sticky as the glue kept in the art box.

Mr. Vincent Wilson, the headmaster, had been made aware that everything at his school, living or not, was melting like the ice lollies he had been forced to buy and supply. Even if they had got there, by the time the students were free to go to the canteen at lunch, they would be nothing but lolly sticks swimming around in frozen fruit juices: Not fit for eating. And not worth drinking.

Despite Mr. Wilson's efforts, it was not enough to stem the torrents of sweat. One such morning, before the toaster oven of a school, was set to open, an emergency board meeting was called with Mr. Wilson and his peers. Multiple complaints were brought up, however, there was extraordinarily little he could say. Despite the common consensus to keep up appearances at the school, even the staff were forced to wear casual clothing at this meeting. Hence why Mr. Wilson was wearing a pair of denim jeans and a stripy t-shirt.

'This is impossible to put up with, ladies and gentlemen,' He commented. 'The summer heat is impossible to measure and deal with. Anyone would think we were working in a massive furnace. This is no way to work. For the students and us.'

'You mean to say this heat is worse than the Beast from the East?' Mr. Goodman asked.

'I'm afraid so, George,' Mr. Wilson confirmed. Mr. Goodman was an influential member of staff: Mr. Wilson's deputy headmaster. He, too, was wearing casual clothes, however a thin jacket over a Hawaiian shirt to show he was still in a position of authority.

'If you haven't noticed, George, it's getting hotter day by day,' Mr. Wilson stated. 'I don't see how we are not on the floor already.'

'Yes, but what can you do about it?' Another member of the teaching staff, Mrs. James, asked. She was a determined mathematics teacher dressed in a business dress with a pair of glasses on her face. 'You have a serious responsibility to our students, Vincent. We need to make sure our students are cooled down before any of them faint. Remember Phillip Bridges last week?'

The headmaster felt genuinely concerned about what he was being told. 'I appreciate the concern, Ella. There is only so much that one person can do'.

Young Phillip Bridges. Phil for short. He was a disabled student at the high school. Ever since he had been born, he had been visually impaired if other words, blind. He could be often seen wearing a pair of tinted glasses over his clouded eyes, and a yellow cane he used to tap out the floor in front of him. For most of his life at school, learning was hard for him to do. He found it hard to learn and read braille, and carers were not easy to come by.

Phil found himself to be on his own for long gaps in time and found it hard to fit in with the rest of his students. Many of his classmates, who had sight, felt sorry for his disability and how it had adverse effects on his life and his learning environment. Now that the boy was now in Year Eleven, and with lots of exams coming around the bend, things were bound to become even worse for him.

But, for what his permanent disability had done to Phil his whole life, there is something hidden beneath the surface.

A new boiling day was dawning over the school. Another load of exams was about to happen. An attractive young man, dressed in a crisp school uniform, called Wesley Devon, arrived at the school social area. His brown hair was combed neatly and tidy. His moustache was smart and clean. His face was washed clean, and he looked fresh. His exams had just got going: Already, he had had his English exams and his history test.

These had been good for him as part of his options. Previously, he had excelled in his science exams and had enjoyed leaving a difficult subject behind. Presently, he had been in school for much of the morning to revise for the morning's math exam. Other members of his year group were around the premises to see him: They had been up at the same time and had enjoyed revising the last few hours away.

'What a busy morning this has been today,' Wesley observed as he sat down for a last-minute breakfast: A bacon sandwich with brown sauce squeezed inside. 'It hasn't even started yet. The heat outside hasn't been helpful. I swear to God, if Mrs. James turned down the Air Conditioning any lower, anyone would think we were the North Pole'.

Wesley then looked up to see a female student who arrived through the closed door to him. Her name was Hailey Southerland. She was a sweet, optimistic girl with golden brown and smooth-looking skin. Her smile through her pink lip-gloss brightened Wesley's expression as he maintained his eye contact on her as she sat down in front of him.

'You look like you're not comfortable with the next exam,' She sensed.

'I not sure how else to feel about this one.' Came the nervous reply.

'I always say that everything will work out in the end, Wes,' Hailey commented. 'You'll be fine. Won't we all?'

'That's easy for you to say,' Wesley retorted indignantly. 'You have two to get through today. It doesn't make sense what you say there. You have two, and I only have one'.

'I feel like this regardless of how many,' Hailey smiled confidently. 'I will let you know how it turns out a little later.' Hailey was quite exuberant in her manners. Very over the top for a person her age, nevertheless a well-meaning attitude. This was seen for her always having a rich smile on her face. 'I will see you in maths in 10 minutes,' She said as she got up from the table. She took off and ran out of the canteen to the exam hall.

Wesley was left on his own for a while. The canteen was now so silent you could hear a pin drop on the other side: You could listen to it drop even before it hit the floor. Wesley had already eaten half of his sandwich. He was just getting stuck into the other half, and the door opened again close to him. In walked another 'friend' of his. This was Gemma Beckett. She was a very tall girl for being the same age as Wesley: 16. She looked strong enough to have her way with anyone. She stood over the young lad. He looked so skinny to her that she could see his ribs. She had been listening to what they had been saying. She was not amused.

'You seriously have to get real, Wes,' she frowned. 'What makes you think you have any chance of going to the prom with Hailey?'

'I don't see a problem with that kind of idea,' Wesley replied. 'I think it is charming if I do go with her.'

'You sound like a great banana when you talk like that,' Gemma scoffed rudely.

'Oh, I am not as great as the type of bananas you're used to,' Wesley spoke to her a subtle insult. Gemma knew its gross meaning and tried hard to ignore it. Wesley continued with the comment 'A little bit of faith goes a long way for a small person like me.'

The vindictive girl raised an eyebrow at the boy's positive behaviour. 'A small boy like you would need a lot more than faith to have her as a date. If you had asked me, I would shudder at the thought of you carrying me around a dancefloor. I would only take you like a pity date to make sure you weren't lonely on such an important night. It's not like people are going to remember you anyway'.

Wesley did not appreciate this kind of attitude towards him. 'Yeah, but they might remember me in a better light than you.' But, in this situation, there wasn't much else he could say. Given that she had the higher ground in her tone, he decided to speak it back to her. 'Take you to the prom? Pull the other one, love. Like that would ever happen. Why would I want to bring the school slut to a prom? How gross do you think I am?'

Gemma's eyes widened at such a comment. In one giant swing, she slapped Wesley across the face. The metal contact on her rings left a severe scratch across the left side of his forehead. 'How dare you!' She scolded crossly. 'How dare you call me that! I am not what you think I am. And, even if you tried to spill that about, no one would believe you'.

Wesley was not convinced at this. 'A lot of people are already convinced of what you get up to at night.' He said out loud. Looking at Gemma from the boy's angle, she was an appalling state. A large girl in size meant everything else was large. Her yellow skirt showed a lot more leg than necessary for her age and more than appropriate for the school environment. The top of her shirt was open to reveal a neckline that would baffle a giraffe. The large impossible cleavage was visible from out of space: Or in the school's case, across the entire building, especially when she stood at a window, looking down at the hockey field.

Gemma furthered more of her words. 'Something bad is going on at this school. And this neighbourhood. You know it, I know it, the staff know it. No one will admit it,' She said. 'The things people say about me might be true. I may attract men like a magnet attracts paperclips, but I do not go around snatching people in the dead of night'. And with that remark, Gemma Beckett turned on her 9-inch-high heels and flounced away. She had never felt so degraded in her life. Her exam was not going to wait for itself.

Young Devon had no idea what to think of that conversation. The only outstanding fact of it was that it had put him off the last part of his bacon sandwich. This made it feel gross as he took another bite. He turned to his right to see his Music teacher, Ms. Ezequiel, standing in a different doorway. She walked over to him. She noticed the nasty mark on his forehead.

'That looks like a nasty mark,' She observed. 'How bad is it?' She asked.

'It looks worse than it feels,' Wesley sighed as he collected himself. 'What is that girl's problem? What else was I supposed to do?'

'You need not worry about that, son,' Ms. Ezequiel calmed. 'People can be cruel. But that isn't anything to do with you. Don't listen to her. She just plays on other people's emotions. You don't have to listen to any of that nonsense'.

Ms. Ezequiel was a kind member of staff. She always looked out for her students and understood what they were going through. She was wearing informal clothes that day: As a matter of fact, she had been wearing them for a long time, given that she and her fiancé were expecting a child. She was seven months pregnant with a baby girl. The bump was now clearly visible under a striped shirt.

'Thanks, Miss,' Wesley smiled. I hope your little one grows up in the future to be a great woman just like you are'.

'I appreciate that,' Ms. Ezequiel smiled sweetly. 'My 5-year-old cannot wait to meet her baby sister. She's been doing well recently and is behaving as all good girls should'. The teacher noticed the time on the clock hung above the serving hatch. The tone in her voice changed too much more urgent. 'You should get a move on now, Wes. Your exam is about to begin. I wish you the best of luck'.

And with that, Wesley rose from his chair. He left the room. Ms. Ezequiel smiled at him as he did so.

The Exam

Wesley ran as fast as he could. He was careful not to be caught by any member of staff for running. As he drew near the exam hall, he could see the classes large and small, getting in lines and registering. One of Wesley's closest friends was arriving as well. His name was Alec Hanks. He was a smart-looking child with a neatly tied necktie. His blonde hair was fluffy, long, and brushed. His cheeks were covered in visible chicken-pox scars from when he had chickenpox aged six years old. Regardless of how shocking they looked on his complexion, his smile looked strong as his abs.

'So, Wes. Are you ready for this exam, old boy?' He asked his friend casually.

'Sure man,' Wesley said. 'I'm as ready as I'll ever be.' He commented with a forced sense of confidence.

'If you have revised as much as I have, then this should just be a walk in the park for you,' Alec stated. 'You seem to think that the last few of these exams have been like that.'

'So where were you this morning? Playing on the X-Box again?' asked Wes. 'Don't think I have forgotten about what happened three months back. Coming into school in your pyjamas. How stupid is that?' Wes laughed.

'How do you know about that?' Alec was alarmed. 'You were in New York when that happened!'.

'So, you admit that happened?' Wesley said.

The confident student knew when he was beaten. To save himself more embarrassment, he gave a wry smile and a snort. 'Hilarious, Wes.' He joined the line of students beginning to follow into the hall. 'Let's go in, smarty-pants,' Alec said.

On that note, all the students had placed their bags in the small hallway outside the large exam room. Once their bags were all piled up in a large clump, the students entered the room as row by row in alphabetical order. It felt like an airport security guard processing passengers: Only, on this occasion, no one was going to be arrested.

Silent and still. The exam hall was enormous, bigger than a football pitch. It sounded as silent as a 1920's black and white film. Not a word could be uttered. Not even under the breath. No other sounds could be made for fear of fearsome eyes towering over you.

Wesley walked the length and breadth of the room. He took his seat in the middle. Around him was an interesting collective of students: There was his friend Alec, Phil and a small girl called Jade Carlton. She was a sweet young girl with brown hair in a tiny plait. Her nails were a gold colour and her skin smooth. Nerves tingled through her body as she looked at the paper.

The exam invigilators explained the firm rules and regulations of the exam. Sure enough, it was time for the exam to begin. Quick as a car, a bell rang out throughout the room. The time started. Over 300 pages turned over at lightning speed. Over 300 pens clicked, and the caps came off as the exam was set into motion. The pens contacted the papers. The questions were not easy; they looked fearsome for reading and answering correctly.

Wesley got stuck into the examination at great speed. He seemed to be doing very well, and the long-term revision had increasingly paid off for his knowledge. He had just turned over the 14th page when he heard a funny noise in his left ear. *'You will pay.'* He stopped dead in his tracks. What was that noise? What could it mean? He decided to carry on writing the next few questions.

These seemed to be challenging for a student of his ability. Then, he heard the strange sound again. *'You will pay for what you did to me.'* Wesley stopped writing again. Another funny noise in the room above. He was beginning to feel rather scared. Beginning to feel if someone was watching him from somewhere in the room. Wesley Devon looked all the way around him at the entire room. The sound had disappeared. It also didn't look like there had been anyone watching either.

Then, he heard a different noise in his ear again—the advance of smartly polished shoes brushing across the wooden floor. Wesley turned back to his desk to see an adult wearing casual clothes under a thick formal jacket. It was the deputy head, Mr. Goodman. He knelt down to his level and spoke sincerely, calmly, and quietly.

'Do you think you could keep your head still, please?' He asked seriously. 'Your movements around this seat are very distracting,' He stated quietly. Wesley sat very still: As if there was a wasp in the room that only he was aware of. The deputy finished off with a calm tone of speech. 'If you are hot, son,' He concluded. 'You should take your jumper off.' He did so right away and put it behind his chair. 'Do not make me come over here again, boy. They'll be hell to pay'. He warned with a serious frown.

The teacher walked away, sternly back to the front. Wesley felt the seriousness of the situation he had caused. He picked up his pen and set to writing again.

It was coming to the end of the examination. There was only half an hour left on the clock. People were still writing at this time: Either this or they had just given up on the exam. Wesley was feeling great discomfort inside himself. He was one question away from finishing the test. It was an algebra question involving lots of complex symbols.

This one had him scratching his head intensively: As if he were a cat sharpening his claws on the back of a sofa. The heat was intense as well. It was becoming more impossible to deal with. Wesley had found that even taking off his jumper as ordered had not helped a lot. Nervously, he raised his right hand slowly as to raise attention. One of the invigilators noticed it and advanced in his direction.

'What's the matter?' He hissed.

Wesley plucked up enough courage to speak in silence. 'I need to go to the toilet.' He finally said.

The invigilator knelt and spoke. 'Do you have a toilet pass?' He asked. Wesley shook his head slowly. 'You're going to have to wait until the end of the test. Fortunately, you only have 25 minutes. Can you wait?'

'I think so,' Wesley whispered.

The invigilator nodded. 'I will remember, and you can leave first in this row.' The invigilator walked away respectfully.

The 25 minutes spoken of passed like clockwork. Suddenly, the bell that started the exam rang again. Mr. Goodman spoke into a microphone so he could be heard all the way around.

'Ok, students,' he addressed. 'Could you please stop writing. Your time is finished'.

The countless number of students put down their pens. The exam was finally over. Wesley breathed a heavy sigh of relief. He knew all too well the exam was over. The booklets were quickly collected in row by row. An invigilator approached Wesley Devon and let him get up for the bathroom. He sauntered away. As he was moving, the rest of the hall was being cleared as before when the students were entering.

Wesley Devon kept his eye on the exam room until the last moment. Just to be sure only the remaining students and staff were watching.

The Bathroom

This is where the bizarre chain of events and actions began to unfold and develop into sinister shapes and signs. Not many people would escape with their minds intact.

Wesley Devon left the exam hall feeling incredibly happy for himself. However, for all the sense of pride, he still felt quite queasy inside. This uneasiness made him very unaware and unprepared for what was to follow inside the boy's toilets. Already, he had come out of the room before his students. As he walked into the bathroom, he could hear the steps of them walking out of the exam hall now. Wesley thought he would calm himself down in the toilet first before joining them at the far end of the school.

Inside the toilet, he seemed to be the only person there. While looking all around the lavatory, he strolled into the far cubical. Now that he was inside it, he closed and bolted down the door so that no one would enter and disturb him.

Wesley Devon proceeded to do his private business. It seemed to be rather motionless. All of a sudden, several things started to happen. Above Wesley was a long bar of yellow light hanging and swinging above his head. It suddenly began to flicker on and off. It was like a faulty torch flickering around an attic.

Wesley began to feel very suspicious. He was certain he was the only person in the room. Could there be someone in here too playing with the switch? Still looking up and just finishing off using the toilet, he called out, 'Is someone in here?'. There was no answer. Maybe they left before he could say something. Wesley spoke out again. 'Stop playing with the lights, please?' He asked politely but nervously. There was still no answer. Both content and discontent at this, Wesley proceeded to wipe himself with toilet paper from the holder. He pulled up his trousers.

Wesley stood up off the toilet seat. He thought everything weird had ended. There would be worse to come. He was about to pull the toilet chain. That was when he saw an even stranger sight. A large black human shadow began to crawl under the door towards him. Wesley started to think several things at once. It was as if someone would open the door on him. This would feel strange, regardless of whether Wesley was finished or not. The awkward image was trying to mess with his sense and nerves all over.

'J-j-j-j-j-just give me a moment,' Wesley stuttered. 'I won't be too long.' He feared something would happen. He reached out his left arm towards the toilet chain. He was in touching distance. He breathed deeply, keeping an eye on the shadow. He shut his eyes for a brief moment, spun his whole body around, and flushed the chain. The drums made the common flush noise, and the waste disappeared down the pipes. Wesley turned back, expecting the shadow to be there still. But it was not. The shadow had disappeared. As if no one had been there in the first place.

Wesley's heart skipped a beat. He dreaded an idea that whoever the shadow belonged to was behind the cubicles waiting to jump out on him. Still, he couldn't stay in the toilet all day, or the teachers would get worried. So, coolly as possible, he opened the door and walked out of the bathroom. He walked towards the sink to wash his hands. As he was doing so, he saw that nothing else was in the bathroom. The light switch was unattended. No other shadows others than his were there. Wesley began to feel very embarrassed. At this stage, he decided to leave the bathroom. He thought that it would be better he did not say anything until he reached the other end of the school with the others. However, he did not trust himself in that comment.

'Don't be an idiot, Wes,' he stammered quietly to himself. 'Even the smartest kids have an off day. Once in a while. For some reason. I don't know,'. Wesley walked out of the boy's toilet. He was glad he was ok in there. But, if he had looked behind before leaving the bathroom, he would've seen a pair of strange orange objects hovering on the wall.

Gradually, having grabbed his bag and shook himself down, Wesley began to pick up the pace and run for it. He heaved his long way to join the rest of his improbable friends. He burst into the cafeteria. He saw his mathematics teacher Mrs. James sitting at a bench. She looked as if she had been waiting for him. 'At last!' She exclaimed as the boy finally made eye contact with her. 'You took your time!' She changed her barking to a more questioning tone. 'So, how was your exam, Wesley?'

Wesley was in a state of mind of his own. So much so, he had not heard the question at all. He was still reflecting on the bizarre event that he had encountered in the bathroom. Mrs. James decided to reinforce herself. 'Your exam, Wesley?' She barked. 'How did you think it went today?'

Wesley finally came too. He spoke off the cuff for his answer. 'It was a surprisingly good exam. For maths, I suppose'. Before Mrs James had a chance to ask another question, Wesley Devon took off again. He ran down the length of the cafeteria. 'WALK, DON'T RUN!' Mrs. James called after him. Wesley slowed down. He now began to walk away.

The young lad walked out of school, onto the wasteland of a playground. It was another blazing day. Wesley looked around the playground until he finally saw Alec standing near the bike shed. He walked in his direction. Alec took notice and raised an eyebrow.

'You took your time,' he exclaimed. He noticed that his friend was quite pale in his skin. 'Are you alright, Wes?'.

Wesley stared at him with tired eyes. 'It's fine, dude,' He replied. 'Although there might be something I want to talk to you about a little later.'

'That Would Be Fine With Me,' Alec Decided. 'Let Me Know When You Are Ready.'

With this, Wesley decided to make his way to the rear entrance of the canteen. It seemed that everyone was oddly quiet around the premises. This was not normal for the playground. Wesley was quite puzzled. Had they also seen the same things Wesley had? Break time had been at this point. By the time all the students had been released, things had become awkward. Wesley had to make sure he didn't see things in the toilets.

Things seemed to return to the normal pace. But it would not stay normal for long.

The Scream

It was in the afternoon. Things had progressed silently. Wesley had had quite a strange day. He was walking around the school corridors. He looked down the hallways. He stopped at a cross-point that connected 3 of the halls. They looked strongly dark: It was as if he was in a scene from a horror film set in a mental hospital. It was a tense feeling around the passageway.

He then heard a blood-curdling scream coming from where he was standing. It sounded shrill and ear-piercing. He couldn't see anything making the noise. But, he could feel it was coming somewhere from his view.

'What the heck is going on now?' He asked out loud. 'Who did that?' He said. He began making his way towards where he thought the noise came from. He looked around a cloakroom: It appeared to be empty. He turned away from the cloakroom. He glared. He saw the sight of a group of Year 8 boys congregating around a toilet. They were giggling as if they had all drunk a bottle of pop between then. Wesley was not amused at this as he walked in their direction. He gathered a lot of breath in his lungs as he charged up to the doorway.

'HEY!' He barked loudly like a dog. It made the children jump up and react abruptly. They turned to face the Year 11, as he began to tell them off. 'Do you mind. There's an exam going on nearby. Keep it down, will you'. The Year 8 children found themselves to be told. They silenced themselves immediately. Wesley smirked at his commanding manner. He began to turn away from the mob. But then, something else happened that would make his mind think too many things at once.

There came another scream. It was just as loud as he had heard before. It was the sound you would get if you stubbed your toe on a bedpost as you got into bed. Wesley turned around with a frown at the group of boys. He felt very indignant at what he thought he heard.

'Did you not hear me, you lot?' He snapped. 'I thought I had told you to shut the hell up. What are you even doing here behaving like this? This is a...' Wesley found himself silencing. There was more screaming coming from around the area. This time, Wesley was looking at the boys. This time, he could see that they were not making the noise. Their lips were not moving at all.

'What on Earth is going on with this school?' Wesley said out loud with bewilderment.

'What is your problem?' One of the boys asked. 'Are you alright, dude?'

Wesley thought it would be better if he tried to think less of what he was encountering. 'I think you guys should be going,' he advised to the Year 8's. 'Not a word to any of your peers or parents. No one can understand this. Get your backsides out of here'.

There was no hesitation. The children ran past Wesley and raced off as fast as their legs could carry them. The beats of their footsteps were loud enough to wake a sleeping lion from a nap. They could be heard around the hallway. Ms. Ezequiel had heard the loudness over one of her videos. She popped her head around the door to see what the racket was.

'Slow down, you lot. This is not a racetrack,' she scolded. The boys were already long away from her. Ms. Ezequiel was about to close the door. The sight of Wesley standing strangely in the hallway. She opened the door further to see a full better look at him. He was standing as still as the ocean.

'Wesley,' She said. 'What are you doing there?'

Wesley was aware of a teacher talking towards him. He turned towards the sound of her voice. But, he had nothing to say. 'Can you hear me from back there?' Ms. Ezequiel asked. 'Don't you have somewhere you need to be, lad?'

Wesley gave a nervous nod. He walked around the corner and out of sight. The other way that the Year 8's had gone. 'I do hope he's ok,' Ms. Ezequiel thought. She closed the door and returned to her talk.

Wesley had run out of school and stopped. He sat down on a step. Why was all of this happening to him? It seemed to be just him that this was happening. He felt he was alone with the younger year students. How wrong he was. He could hear so many screams at once. The Year 8 students must not have been the only screamers. The realisation was out there to see that there was not only one faction screaming but two.

I guess it makes you start to wonder if Wesley was actually on his own. Visually, that would've been a yes. But, sight can only carry so much. Moreover, another obvious blank in the situation was, why would the teacher be nowhere to be seen? She emerged when three screams had sounded off. And when Wesley had told the children to be silent twice.

It would soon be time for lunch. Wesley hoped that nothing else would happen. Too many weird things had happened already: He couldn't understand half of them. If Wesley could, and if he had the speed for it, he would run around the entire school premises. He would do this until his legs could not take another step. He would practically do anything that would keep him away from anything stupid. The adrenaline levels of a man his age had never been higher. They were even higher and worse than what they were in the bathroom and the exam room. This was not normal at all.

Wesley eventually made his way to his history class. He knocked on the door. The response was an opened door with the headmaster, Mr. Wilson, there in front of him. 'There you are, Devon,' he reacted. 'Where on Earth have you been?' He asked. 'You had me worried sick. Get inside at once'. He ordered. Wesley did as he was told and walked through to see a lot of student bodies fixed on him. As he walked in, a terrible haunting pair of eyes stared at him from across the hall. Only there for a second, then merely vanishing into dust right in front of his very eyes. He sat down without a word for the remainder of the lesson.

It wasn't too long before word got out to the rest of the school. Soon, nearly everyone had heard what Wesley had seen and been involved with. Wesley caught up with a lot of his peers. One of these was the younger sister of Hailey, Rebecca, or Becca for short. She was a smart young lady, two years younger than Hailey. She was a brilliant young child with golden sun-kissed skin and black hair. Her uniform was neat, and her lips were a natural colour.

'That scream had to have come from something.' Becca said after listening to Wes's story. The idea did not convince her of a haunting. 'Screams that loud do not come from out of thin air. Surely you must know that, dude'.

Wesley was not convinced at the idea of logic. 'There was one scream. It sounded like it was from the children. I told them to be quiet. Then there was another. I thought that was one of them behind my back. I told them to be quiet again. Then there was more screaming. Can you explain how that works, Becca?'

'Well, there had to be a voice somewhere nearby,' Becca was still adamant about logical sense. 'You and those boys were not by yourselves.'

'If there was someone else,' Wesley began to theorise for himself. 'I think I probably would've seen them too.'

Devon then heard someone behind him clear their throat. It turned out to be Alec. He had been eavesdropping nearby. He was standing in the archway of the bike shed and had been watching closely and listening to every word. Wesley saw the look on his face and sensed it didn't feel like he had a nice thought in his mind. Wesley invited him into the conversation. He felt there was something he needed to hear from his close friend.

'What is it, Alec?' He asked. 'Is there something you know?'

'I think so,' Alec considered. 'I might know what you are talking about.'

'What makes you say that Al?' Wesley enquired. 'How do you mean?' Alec spoke.

'Wes, have you ever wondered why no one had been put in the isolation room for almost five years? Because the students of this school are not all well behaved'.

Wesley thought there was a lot of truth in this statement. Becca slunk away quietly. She walked until she was directly out of sight of the curious boy. But, her ears remained sharp as ever. She had not entirely left the area. For her ears were about to pick up some lethal information.

Three other students emerged to join the conversation. These being Jade, Hailey, and Phil. Hailey had her arm on Phil so she could guide him across the premises. Jade had heard enough to put forward her views. 'I am gonna guess that it is something that no one around this school, or this neighbourhood, talks about.' She said.

The old isolation room was on the top floor of the school. It had been emptied for as long as any of Wesley's year could remember. Of course, they were not there when it closed down.

'It is something unspoken,' Phil agreed. 'Ever since the fatal accident up there.'

Wesley's ears rang with shock. 'Fatal accident?' He gasped. 'S-s-s-someone died up there.'

'Yes,' Phil agreed.

'Did someone fall from the window?' Alec asked.

'No,' Phil denied. 'Far worse. Alec, tell him the story'.

'Story. What story?'

Alec sat down a bench. He cleared his throat and began to spin a dreaded tale of woe, evil, and death.

'It was a long, long time ago at this school. There was this student. He couldn't have been more than 13/14. I don't know what his name. Or what he looked like. But, what I do know is that he was one of the most disturbed kids ever. They say he never smiled. He always seemed to have a haunting look on his face. The staff kept him up at the far end of the school. They said his behaviours was far too scary for the younger years. So scary that he made one of the Year 7's cry…'

'Who is this kid?' Wesley interrupted.

'For heaven sakes, dude, I just told you that,' Alec growled. 'I don't know what he looks like. Or what his name was. No one did. But, one thing I can say: His eyes were glowing red. They looked like balls of fire. Can you please let me finish!'

'Continue,' Wesley said.

Alec carried on with his story. 'The boy's behaviour was incredibly maniacal. He would throw random students' rucksacks down stairwells. He would purposely kick glass windows with his boots until they shattered. He would stab people with knives he brought into school. He would set the toilet buildings on fire using light switches and petrol. He would bring weed into school and dish it out to the younger years.'

The people around him listening to the story were looking at him with the most shocked faces. They had never heard such horrid accounts.

'Many members of staff were scared of his actions. They would not dare to approach him at the risk of being a victim to his horrid campaign. That fact was especially apparent when he started massive scale fights in the school playground. The result was hardly pleasant. One such fight ended up with a little girl losing the use of her right hand. Eventually, after the mayhem and havoc, he had caused, the headmaster ordered that he be placed in permanent isolation. Never to be let out again.

The boy was condemned to watch over the school from atop that building. Everyone felt there was something wrong with that kid. Some say he was created by none other than The Devil himself. The boy stayed up in the room for the longest time ever. He watched everyone work and play from atop that tower. The haunting evil red eyes greeted those who were forced to walk past the room. His eyes struck fear into anyone he looked at. There he stayed for days and weeks on end.

But then, one afternoon, it happened…'

'What did he do?' Jade asked, becoming more convinced.

'Did he break out?' Wesley asked.

'He did not escape,' Alec denied.

'Did he run away?' Phil asked.

'There would not have been anyway for him to run away. Or anywhere for him to have gone to. The door was locked'.

'Did he kill himself?' Hailey asked.

'Nothing of the sort,' Alec said. 'It was something far worse than that. I can remember seeing the fire'.

'Fire?' Wesley never felt more switched on than his life. More switched on than his mobile phone during lessons.

'I remember hearing about this too,' Phil recalled. 'Can I tell him?' He asked.

'Go ahead,' Alec permitted.

Phil described the boy's fate.

'No one is entirely sure what caused the blaze. One afternoon, in the isolation room, there was a massive fire. It covered the entire room. It burst into flames on all sides. The headmaster ordered the whole tower block to be evacuated. A fire crew was called to the scene of the devastation. But it was already too late. The boy and the room were already going up in smoke. In flames, they could not see him anymore. But, what they did see were a pair of angry red eyes staring at them before they crumbled into ashes.

The room was completely burnt to the ground. They cleared the flames away to see charred remains of a scorched room. They could not find any human remains. It appeared he had been burnt down. All that was left, however, was the fragments of a human skull'.

'So, he died in the fire,' Wesley observed.

'That's what some people think,' Alec commented. 'No one can be sure whether he survived or not. Of course, his physical self was destroyed in the inferno. But some say his spirit endured the pain'.

'What do you mean?' Hailey asked.

Alec continued the story onto a familiar event. 'About a year passed. Things had been normal for a while. Whatever was left of the boy was laid to rest in a nearby graveyard. Then, things started to change drastically. People began to disappear. It began with a rainy night with two workers busy on a canal. One of them had noticed a pair of hovering amber objects near the edge. He went up there to investigate. When he came back to his co-worker, he was shattered with fear.

He claimed the pair of objects had been a set of blazing red eyes. No one believed what he said. So, he took some people up to the spot to get a better look.

And that, my friends, is where it ends. None of those who went up to the riverbank were ever seen or heard from again. Since that disappearance, people had lived in fear around the neighbourhood. There have been many similar cases of people coming across the Eyes in a dark place of fear. But, not all have lived to tell the tale.

There were once rumours of someone in a large van driving in the dead of night across an old iron bridge. He was driving along a weak road and very misty. It was suggested that he had caught sight of The Evil Eyes somewhere. He lost himself and lost control of his vehicle. He braked hard, but there was nothing that could be done to save him from what came next. The weakened road gave way from underneath him, and he plunged over the side into the murky oozing swamps below. Local authorities were alerted, but the van had already sunk, taking the guy to a watery grave. They dug around in the water. They found his body covered in muck and scum. But, the van he was travelling in was nowhere to be seen'.

Alec finished off the story in one last haunting sentence. 'So, always remember friends, no matter where you are in the world, there is always someone watching you.'

The story ran very deep through the ears and minds of the audience. After the telling of it had concluded, they were left as still as the oceans. Their jaws were dropped so low. You could fit a rolled-up pair of socks in their mouths. The stillness of those in attendance was disrupted violently by the ringing of the school bell. The students could think of nothing else but to go to their next lessons and not be a minute late.

Many questions ensued about the story that had been told. The students wondered how this Devil Student could have existed the way it had. How could the school not know who he was or his appearance? Also, how could he have burnt up in that fire on that afternoon when the room was empty?

Furthermore, the students began to question each other. How did Alec know about the boy? How did Phillip Bridges know the circumstances of the boy's death? It all sounded too impossible to comprehend.

'Devil Student?' Caitlynn thought to herself. She thought ridiculously hard and disregarded a lot about the legend. She was a child who didn't feel a lot about supernatural stories. Yet, for all her opinions, she still felt amazed that someone could be capable of the atrocities. 'You'd think you know somebody. How does something like that happen in common society?' But, all the same, she kept thinking and wondering about the story. How much of it was true? She thought this all of the day, even after school.

But the students will soon find out that they are the story. And there remained more troubles on the horizons. For everyone they cared about as well as each other.

The Nightmare

This is where Hailey's sweet and innocent younger sister, Becca, fully comes into our story. You may remember her from earlier when Wesley was talking to her about the strange voices in the hallway. She was as sweet as her older sibling Hailey. Caring, confident, and happy was her natural state. Unknown to the Year 11 students, she had been listening to the haunting tale. What she had heard was incredibly fearsome, mysterious, and completely disturbing for a girl in Year 9. Sadly, for her curiosity, her wondering ears would pay a heavy price for getting involved in the older children's lives indirectly. A price costly in the way of sanity.

That evening, the Southerland family had had a takeaway from the shop in the next street. A Chinese meal that consisted of noodles and spicy meats. After eating the spicy foods, the four of them, parents and both girls, sat down in front of the TV to watch the film 'The Wizard of Oz.' It was the mum's choice of film, stating it was one of her favourites. The dad, slightly withdrawn by musicals, still felt like singing at the song sequences. The family felt he did a sweet rendition of 'Over the Rainbow.'

As common for the family, they were quickly in bed when it was dark. The parents had their bedroom for themselves. Both of the sisters had their separate rooms. They were both opposite each other and both close to the bathroom. It was nine-thirty at night when the last person, Hailey, finally settled down for bedtime. The lights had finally gone out. The house was utterly pitch black. It felt so quiet you could hear a rat crawling across the floor around the skirting boards.

But this peace was not going to last. The ghostly winds rattled outside the house like a washboard cleaning grease off a plate. It was only going to be getting worse from then on.

And, for the rest of their lives, nothing would ever be the same.

It was one o'clock in the morning. The first hour of the day was complete. It was at this point that the nightmare truly began to morph. It started with Becca shaking herself among the covers of the bed, trying to get comfortable in an otherwise comfy bed. She was tossing and turning all over the bed and making bizarre moves on the single mattress. Her breathing now began even faster and heavier and louder. It was as if she was drowning in a swimming pool. The silence around her in the blackness was incredibly toxic.

After a small while of trying to make herself comfortable, Becca firmly gave up. She opened her bright eyes. The whites of her eyes and the vibrant colour were visible in the horrid blackness of her room. She sat upon the top of the bed and scratched her head. She looked out into the dark to see if anything was going on: Whether there was something on the floor; Or if there was something against the window; There appeared to be not. She could not see anything in the thickness of her room. The natural pink of her wallpaper was replaced by the blackness hidden by the light turned off. All the while, she kept wondering what was making her behave this way. What was going on around her in the black space?

Then, she saw them. They were a very faint image portrayed at the end of her bedpost. She rubbed her eyes at the sight. They opened up slowly. These were two hovering objects. They seemed to have come out of nowhere—coloured red in their appearance. Black dots were invading the red space portrayed. Becca began to tremble with fear at what she was witnessing. Then, she could hear a loud demonic laugh: The kind you'd listen to from a classic film from a villain. The objects zoomed in to see that they were a pair of The Evil Eyes.

'AAAAAAAAAAAAAAAARRRRRRRRRRRRRRRR
RRGGGGGGGGGGGGGGGGGGGGGHHHHHHHHHHHHHH
!!!!!!' Becca let out an ear-splitting scream all around her
bedroom. It was so loud it made the entire house shake all
over. The scream was powerful enough to awaken the houses
that were either side of the Southerland residence. Her parents and her sister were woken suddenly by the actions. They
responded quickly, both jumping out of bed quickly and rac-
ing towards the scene of distress. They ran towards the room:
As the shrieks of fear raged on inside the room.

The dad, in such a state beyond thinking, kicked open the
door while wearing his pyjamas and only one of his yellow
slippers. He dived inside, flicking a light switch on the way
in. By doing this fast action, a large glow of orange light entirely flooded Becca's room. Despite this, no difference
could be made at all. They found the youngest sibling cowering all over the bedspread, covered up under the bed quilt.
Both Hailey and her mum raced to her side to relax her.

'Hey! Hey! Listen to us!' The mother pleaded. Becca froze
on the bed. The mother proceeded to speak some more.
'Becca stop all of this, please child. Calm down!' Becca
heard the urgency in her voice. She ceased in the loud noises
of her screaming panic attack.

Becca took a deep breath of fresh air. She began to turn her
head towards the rest of her family. A small trickle of tears
flowed down her face, most of them hitting her pillows. The
father tried not to see as he handed her the tissue he kept
under his pillow. Becca's beautiful eyes were filled so much
trauma and dread. She was sweating and shaking all over.

'What in God's name happened to you?' Hailey enquired as
she sat down on the bed. She put her arm around her sister.
'You can tell us. We're all around you; you are calm'. Becca
tried to swallow her fear and speak of her panics. But it was
not easy for her to communicate in her damaged state of

mind. All that could be heard were an odd collection of stutters. They sounded like the noise you'd get on a broken CD player jammed on a song.

'T-t-t-t-t-there was a-a-a-a-a-a...' She uttered with no conviction whatsoever. She tapped her chest slowly as to get the air to flow to her lungs. She looked incredibly pale in her skin. She looked like she would fall unconscious on the bedspread.

'Slow down, child,' The mother calmed. 'Take your time. What are you trying to tell us?'

Becca finally managed to finish her sentence correctly. 'A-a-a-a terrible face.' Was finally said. Becca pointed her long arm towards the end of the bed, towards the glass window. It was covered in beautiful decorative objects, hanging from the windowsill.

'A face, you say?' The dad considered. 'Here? You must have been seeing things.'

'I do not doubt what I saw,' the girl protested. 'Right over in that corner over there. A pair of evil red eyes. I heard a laugh among them. Right there! Staring at me!'

The parents and older sister were alarmed at what they were being told. 'You cannot be serious. Eyes? In here'.

'You have to believe me, guys,' Becca pleaded for recognition of what had happened.

'We do believe you,' Hailey sympathised. 'What did these Eyes look like?' Hailey began to feel that the Eyes in her sister's bedroom were the same referred to as the story told by both of her friends.

'Red. As red as sin.' She described in full view. 'They looked red. They also looked orange'. With this description,

Hailey's worst fears had been realised. The Eyes were real, after all.

'I could hear a laugh as well,' Becca said as she continued her words of horror. 'It sounded horrible in its tone and whatnot. It completely made me scream the house down, as you may have heard all over. I'm not kidding you guys. There is something out there. And you know it'. She took another breathe in and out.

'I heard your story. It's coming for me'.

Her family had no idea how to feel at what was unfolding. Her dad finally put a kind and caring hand on his daughter's forehead. It was scorching. 'Shush. Shush. There's no need for you to be scared now. Look to my face. Do not fret for you will be ok. There's nothing in here now. Just continue to keep breathing in and out. who's my brave girl?'

Becca felt very reassured in what she was being told. She took a very deep breath in her lungs. Her big brilliant sister came around to her angle to give her a massive hug.

'Do you feel any better, lass?' The mum asked.

Becca nodded very slowly. 'I'm beginning to feel a whole lot better now than what I was.'

The dad smiled as he looked at his daughter's room. He could not believe what he was looking at. In his child's struggle, there were a lot of objects that had been thrown around all over the place. To quote a common phrase, the room looked like 'a bomb had hit it.' One of the said objects that had been displaced was the mirror that was on the girl's makeup desk. It had been pushed over and had landed on the floor. The mum looked at the mirror that had ended up being knocked sideways. She said: 'Let me put this the right way up for you, darling.' She lifted the framed mirror and placed it back on the desk. She put it up there to see a pretty face.

But, that was not the thing she would visualise in the glass framing. What she would see in the mirroring was something that would make any person question their sanity. It made her blood run cold as the waters of the North Pole. There, in the reflected glass background, just above the wardrobe, there flickered both of the Evil Eyes. They opened in a way that a person would open them up after blinking.

The mother was shocked at such a sight as this.

'Uhm… Scottie…' She shuddered as she called for her husband.

'Yes, love,' the husband responded to his wife. 'What is it, honey?' He turned to her direction to see what the worry was. 'What is the matter?'

His wife, Grace Josie Southerland, pointed towards the mirror and brought him in close in a confident hope he was would see what she had. But, when he turned across to gaze at the mirrored glass window, there were no other eyes for him to see.

The husband looked back to his wife with a very disturbed and significantly confused expression on his face.

'Whatever is it, love?' He asked in a concerned tone. 'Whatever did you see? Because I cannot see anything other than a beautiful group of women'.

Grace continued to be pointing at the mirrored glass where she had seen The Eyes. Something was seriously bugging the dad as he surveyed what was going on in such a tiny bedroom.

'You must be seeing things!' the dad screeched, his name being Scott Lucas Southerland. The tone in his voice changed to being irritated. The fact that he was being drawn into these stressful moments was not doing well for his sleep pattern. And given that he was up past midnight, this did not do any other favours.

'All of you have to be seeing things,' he snapped loudly as the anger in his voice began to filter through the calm reserved person he was earlier when talking to his daughter. 'This is all childish bullshit. We all should be in bed this minute. You lot are seriously too old for all of this childishness.

'Calm the hell down, dad,' Hailey protested. A sense of fear in her voice seeped through as she tried to defuse a deadly situation in her home. 'Do you not see that this is only making it worse for all of us. For all of us, not just my sister and not just you'.

The dad's outburst was strong enough to shake the entire room. At this point after it, Becca was no longer facing anyone. She had now curled up into a ball on the bedspread. All of these arguments going on in her head were causing her great emotional stress and pain in her stomach. A small, sad, and watery tear trickled down her cheek. Everyone felt that there was a distressing feeling for them all in the bedroom.

At long last, the dad calmed himself down with several deep breaths. He had realised that his reaction had not been appropriate. He decided that the family should rest for the night. At this point, it had all become way too much for people like them to handle. All of the family headed back to their respected rooms. The rest of the night looked like nothing before had happened in the first place. Unusually silent. Not a word. Not a sound. No motions were heard at all. Not even a pin drop.

But, for everyone in the family, and the neighbourhood for that matter, it would all become clear that the dad was utterly wrong about what he had initially denied about his views of The Eyes. Had it been real? Was it all just a trick of the light? We shall see.

The Open Road

The night passed quickly enough. The weekend was beginning fast. In the morning, the family found themselves to be going about their regular daily business. Things seemed to be normal for a day, especially given how scary and strange the night had been for the Southerland household. The two sisters, Hailey and Becca, spent their Saturday morning chilling out. Becca had a small portion of homework to do. Thankfully, she had done it the afternoon before; that way, there was nothing to worry about. Grace was up in the kitchen at the ironing board. There was a large impossible pile of clothes in the washing bowl: Almost as high as the roof. It was made up of a majority of the girl's clothes and the father's golf outfits. She hoped that it would all be done by lunchtime so the table would be cleared.

As for the dad, he had a great deal of work to do at his Saturday job. There was a lot of work he had to attend to. His Saturday job consisted of working at a nearby building site, laying up the foundations. It was long hard work, but it paid well for him and his family. He took his old jeep out on the country lanes. He hoped that he would be finished soon so he could return home for his lunch back at home with the family. They were likely to have sandwiches for lunch and then have something hot for dinner.

It was at this point that Scott would encounter a real supernatural thing that could not be possible. He found himself not believing the incidents first hand. He was about to be proved foolishly wrong about what he thought and what he would encounter in the outdoors. A man in his position could not afford mishaps behind the wheel. Sadly, he would not be exempt.

The road he was driving on was extremely bumpy under the tyre treads. Scott grabbed the wheel tight and refused to let it go any other way. It was an incredibly uneven road with the car being pulled all over the road from one side to the other. It was as if the car itself was a thick coil of rope in a Sports Day game of Tug of War. Scott had been down this route many times before when taking the trip to and from work. When talking to his wife and daughters at the table in the afternoon, he had often compared the country roads to riding on a bouncy house inside a rollercoaster car: Too fast and too uncomfortable to put up with. Not an easy route, yet it had to be taken to get to the building site.

Scott's jeep then came to a sharp bend in the road. The black and white arrowed sign showed this, and the van's speed slowed down. Scott then turned the steering wheel hard, and the jeep took a tight deviation to the right. In front of him was a long, wide, and clear open road. The speed of the vehicle picked up again. To Scott's right, there was a massive body of water. It stretched off for miles down the lane. This was the county canal—one of the most beautiful sites in the neighbourhood. However, Scott was not going to find something nice here today. Many people loved to come here to fish and find themselves. It was perfectly motionless, looked to be a peaceful area. His vehicle pressed on.

Then, he saw it. Scott peered into the front windscreen. In the distance, ahead of him, it looked like, from where he was sitting, someone was standing in the middle of the road. He began to slow down the car as quickly as he could. He pulled up on the side of the road in a safe place. Slow but sure, the jeep came to a complete stop. Scott then pulled up the handbrake and switched off the engine.

'What on Earth is going on here?' He spluttered. He had not seen anything like this before. He looked again towards the front. But, when he did so, it appeared that there was no longer a person. Scott had become extremely puzzled at what was forming.

He got out of the jeep, opening the door, jumping down, and locking the door behind him. He walked a long way ahead of the large vehicle. He made his way up to the area where he saw the figure standing alone, the figure that made him stop in the first place. As he made his wary advance towards the same area, he felt the world begin to change around him mysteriously. Something was going wrong. It seemed to be getting hotter and colder, both at the same time.

'What is going on with this place?' Scott asked himself in awe. He was sensing the feeling that he was not by himself. He called out into the clear world. 'WHO'S THERE!'

No one answered the yell he made. He looked around the location. There seemed to be no one. No one there for miles and miles. Scott peered down into the riverbank. Still nothing. He was beginning to feel a little irritated at this hold-up.

'Oh, to bloody blazes with this piece of shit!' He said at long last. 'This tomfoolery has made me late enough as it is. My boss will not believe anything, I say'.

Giving upon his senses, the dad made his way back to his vehicle. He put the key in the hole and started it upright. By correctly moving the pedals, he moved off from the side of the road. He moved slowly and smoothly, keeping his awareness going. However, his hearing was not with him: For when he had got further, he heard a peal of strange evil laughter coming from somewhere close by.

'HAHAHAHAHAHAHAHAHAHAHAHAHAHA!'   The sound of the laugh echoed around the canal. Scott's heart skipped a beat when he heard it. He braked hard enough to stop the car. He could not believe what this was. To make sure he was not crazy himself, he sneaked out a video camera from the glove compartment. He turned it on. He pointed it slowly around the area.

'Who was that?' He asked out loud. 'What the bloody hell is going on here? Where are you? Who are you?'.

Up until now, Scott thought he had been talking to himself. He was wrong when he heard a response to his questions. 'I am the mirror of the hell. This is the hell I designed'. Scott trembled at this comment. He looked around for someone talking to him. He must have been hearing something. Then, he saw something that made his blood run cold.

He peered into his side door mirrors. That was the place where he saw the Evil Eyes. The Eyes lit up in on fire all over the mirror screen. A loud ear-splitting scream shattered the glass.

'AAAAAAAAAAAAAAAAAAAAAAAAARRRRRRRRR RRRRRRGGGGGGGGGGGGGGGGGGGGGHHHHHHHHH HHHHHHHHHHHHHHH!!!!'. Scott looked as if he had wet himself. He put his foot down on the pedal hard enough to almost break it. The car raced off at top speed. It was as fast as THE FLASH! He did not stop until he reached the safety of his home.

When Scott initially got back home, his breathing was bizarre and erratic. His family was shocked and surprised, wanting to know what had happened to him today. He poured out everything he had seen, heard, and failed to see. He tried to show them the video recording: Regretfully, the camera was broken; He had dropped it in a rash panic when he saw The Eyes. The family was very scared of what they were being told. There was something wrong with the neighbourhood. What was everyone up against?

The Disbelief

Monday Morning. The weekend had come and gone like any other usually does. The infrequent paranormal activity had rubbed off severely and quickly, yet it had rubbed the Southerland Family the wrong way. The entire family was now forced to take drastic measures to protect each other. The parents were forced to tell their grandparents they could not come anywhere near the area. This was a hard task for them to do, to think of a fair and logical reason was hard without mentioning The Eyes. They were all now aware that there was a demon ghost spirit out there that was plaguing their beloved neighbourhood. The major authorities needed to know what was causing hell.

It was early Monday morning. The four members of the family marched their way through the school. It was just before the lessons would even begin. They called into the headmaster's office. They went there to inform him of the two incidents they had encountered. Mr. Wilson had his deputy take down pages of notes on the family's ordeal. When he heard everything, he had a very extreme reaction to it.

'Bloody hell!' He gasped out loud. 'This sounds incredibly impossible.' The words he had heard and notes he had made him feel very weary. He looked at Becca's face. There was a lot of fear and trauma in her face. 'The poor girl.' He tried to sympathise. 'You look like you have had the wind taken out of you'. He began to rummage through a load of flyers at the end of the desk. 'Don't you guys worry; I have this under control. I shall do everything in my power to protect the children. I have here the numbers for a bucket load of counsellors in the meantime'.

The parents were grateful for the help that was being offered. No one in the office noticed that Wesley was nearby, walking between rooms. He stopped when he heard what was being described. He began to listen in close. Hailey spotted where he was and dragged him over. 'Alright, Wes. Now I know that the story is for real'. She declared the most convincing tone she could try. 'She was listening to what Alec and Phil were on about. I swear to God, if she hears anything else that causes an upset, one demented arsehole is going to get it in the neck'.

'Don't you mean The Eyes?' Wesley asked, trying to calm her down.

'Do not try to be flippant with me,' Hailey snapped again.

'Are you listening to this?' Scott called for his eldest daughter. Hailey came towards him as the father turned back to the headmaster. 'With all due respect, Sir, I do not feel like counselling is going to help my child. It is my firm view that someone is playing a game with us. Whoever it is will have me to answer to, and I will surely be prepared to press criminal charges for it'.

Mr. Wilson was amazed at this man's strong views. 'Are you sure you would want to do that, sir?' He asked nervously. 'What kind of evidence do you have that would suggest someone is messing with you and your family's lives?' The Dad's face began to fall as he began to realise his conviction to have someone sent down was weak. 'The way I see it is that it has been very consistent over the last week. Consistent with me and my girls. There had to be someone messing with us. But it's someone we can't see at all. Does any of this make any sense to you, sir?'

The Headmaster was none the wiser. Wesley Devon decided to present what he knew. He advanced up to the Office door and knocked on it. The family reacted and saw him in the doorway. The Headmaster swung his head in the boy's direction. 'What do you want, Devon?' Mr Wilson asked.

'I might know something about this,' Wesley commented.

'What would it have to do with you?' Grace was truly angry of this intrusion.

'Let him speak,' Hailey calmed.

The Headmaster continued to consult the boy. 'You were saying, son?'.

'A few days ago, I suffered many incidents that would sound similar. I happen to have proof of this'.

'Go ahead then' Wilson allowed. He beckoned his fingers towards the boy, allowing him to enter.

Wesley walked up to the desk. The office room was small for a powerful headmaster. There was a lot of cluttered objects filling the cabinets behind the man in the massive armchair. Bizarrely, there were a couple of glasses at the end of the table with a bottle of whiskey next to them, also made of glass. Wesley described the actions that had occurred while he was in the bathroom, And the hallway.

'So,' Mr. Wilson concluded his views. 'Are you trying to tell me that any person that hears the scary story Alec told you is then effected by The Eye's nightmares?'

'Not just from that, Sir,' Devon noted. 'I only heard the story after what I came across in the boy's toilets and the screams in the hall.' Wesley reminded.

'If that was the case for there,' Wilson commented. 'What makes you so special then? What do The Eyes want with you?'

'I wish I could answer that, sir,' Wesley said. 'Unfortunately, I have no way of knowing.' He let out a dull sigh. 'I guess this family, the children, and I are all connected.'

'Yes. But why?' Hailey questioned. She was beginning to feel more and more alarmed.

Mr. Wilson was thinking some more. He was beginning to feel rather anxious about what was being talked about. 'Does this now mean that I am to suffer these kinds of visions?' He bluntly assumed. 'The last thing I want is for this school to end up as a massive breeding ground for insanity.'

Sensing the urgency of the day, he looked at the clock on his wall. 'It almost form time.' He spoke to the students. 'You guys should be getting off to your form rooms. They should be calling the register. Have a good day, everyone. The receptionist will show the parents out'.

Wesley felt it was a suitable point that they should all leave. The parents exited the school in the same ways they came in. It was firmly declared that no one was to speak a word of what had been witnessed and discussed. Weren't there enough rumours already?

The father was also disappointed that he had been left no choice, but to drop any potential charges. No one was to be arrested or charged. As of right then, they were all on their own and very much in certain doom.

The rest of the day played out as quickly, as regular and as normal as it should do. Wesley, Hailey, and all of the rest of the children went about their nervous work. All the time, the two main teenagers could feel the feeling that the two devil Eyes were watching them from whether any of them lingered. One could be sure: Their world was coming to ruins.

The Devon Household

Often a quiet place at the end of a hard day. That very evening, on the first school night of the week, Wesley Devon was sitting in the front room watching a classical film called 'The Exorcist.' This was a much-loved film regarded to be 'the best horror film ever made.' The front room was completely pitch black, except for an ominous light protruding from the hallway. The horrifying images that the DVD possessed sent a shiver down Devon's spine as he ate his popcorn, one big mouthful after another. The fact that he was in the dark made the atmosphere around him to be utterly horrid and deadly. He had never seen this movie before, and he already doubted the fundamentality of it.

'The story in this thing is ludicrous,' he felt. 'How does a film like this get made? Even in the 1970s. Someone had some serious issues'. But, he was only saying these criticisms to himself.

Or was he?

Wesley Devon was coming up to the mysterious scene with the possessed Regan, the priest had come to see her. As he was watching the moment play out, he felt the loud whistling wind rush against the window. He looked towards the screen as the demonic woman faced out. They were almost eye to eye. As he gazed long and hard, the eyes of the film character seemed to change to a red shade. Wesley felt more hooked than he should be. Did he see things? Was it the videotape having a funny five minutes? He simply couldn't think.

Suddenly, a light bulb from above him flickered on. Wesley shielded his eyes as the yellow bulb light swallowed the blackness of the room. He turned to see his dad, Peter, standing in the doorway. He was a tall man with brown hair, wearing a dressing gown, and carrying a cup of tea.

'What are you doing up this late?' He asked inquisitively. 'I would have thought that the film would have ended by now.' He came into the room further and stood with his back to the door. Wesley turned back to the television screen to see that the red light had vanished. He cleared his throat as he turned off the TV and stood up to face his dad. He was wearing his pyjamas, neatly pressed, and wearing fluffy slippers.

'It is insane all of this ghost stuff,' he said aloud.

'Don't you go and worry about that, son,' his dad said. 'I'm fairly sure it is just a dumb story that one of your friends read off a cereal box'. He looked on the clock above the fireplace. 'Come on now, it's time you were in bed. You can watch more of that film in the afternoon tomorrow. It's amazing how hard you have been working. Keep going, my man'.

Wesley gave his dad a big hug as he ran up the stairs off to bed. His father turned the light off in the hall as he left for his large bedroom.

Wesley had a great deal of respect for his parents. But, he had no idea of a dark secret the family was hiding. One that would betray everything he knew about the people who had brought him up.

The Class

Tuesday. The lesson before lunch was music. That day, Ms. Ezequiel was giving her music lessons. She had little time to go through all of her lessons, given she would be going on maternity leave soon. It had been an incredibly awkward day that day. Devon and several of the girls were in the lesson. Wesley felt incredibly nervous, sitting in the class. From across the room, he could see the storyteller himself, Philip Bridges. He kept a creepy expression towards him throughout the lesson. Wesley began to feel very confused and uncomfortable in his lesson with one of his favourite respected teachers.

Ms. Ezequiel began drawing musical notes on the whiteboard. Given Wesley's inability to draw, these notes were hard to copy off the board. Wesley had an insufficient co-ordination level. His eyes were beginning to become strained as he was bending on the table. Then, as he tried to sharpen his pencil, a funny shape crossed the board. An oval shape appeared and opened up in the light. It was strongly illuminated in the projection screen. Wesley sat very still. As if a snake was crawling up his back. His hand quivered as if he was carrying a plate of cold deserts. The pencil he was sharpening over his workbook shook in his palm and fell from his grasp onto the carpet.

'Pay attention to my words, boy.' The Eye was speaking to him. 'You think it is right for you to deny my existence. You know who I am. You know my name. I go by many of them. All of you will be drowned into the light you selfishly hide in'.

The other Eye floated into position. It appeared in the same projection as it's another Eye. Wesley had never felt tenser in his life. 'So much for watching classic horror movies at night,' he said to himself, under his breath. The large girl who was sitting next to him, Gemma, made a creepy advance to place her large arm on his leg: Right on his right thigh. Wesley Devon reacted as if he had never experienced this touching before in his life. He shook in shock and threw her hand right back at her. He was not happy with this action.

'Gemma, what the hell is your problem?' He asked crossly.

'You dropped your pen, darling,' Gemma retorted in her usual slimy tone. 'Don't worry, laddie. I will get it for you.'

With that offer, Gemma, without second-hand permission, left her class seat to squat down to Wesley's knee level. She ran her hand down his inner leg as she went down. Devon had never felt so embarrassed in his life as Gemma acted in the provocative way she did. Phil and the other members of the class were very aware of what was going on. Eventually, she had clasped the pen, and she crawled back up to the front. She gave Wesley's pen a massive slippery kiss before handing it back. Wesley had never been more repulsed in his life. He pushed the pen and her arm away from him back in her direction.

'On second thoughts, maybe you should keep it.' Instead of saving himself anymore gross imagery, Gemma shrugged her shoulders and placed the pen in her cleavage area. Wesley had never seen anything more repulsive in his life.

Ms. Ezequiel had been aware and had observed the awkwardness of the situation. She tapped the whiteboard with her marker pen to give the boy her full attention.

'Devon, are you paying attention?' She asked. Wesley shook as he sat up properly. He turned his head towards the teacher. He began nodding his head as to say yes. Ms. Ezequiel was not convinced. 'Are you sure, lad? Do you require a moment on your own outside?' She asked.

Devon snapped fiercely. 'No thanks, Ms., I'm fine' came his response.

'Fine, fine,' Ms. Ezequiel relented. 'Just try to stay a bit more focused, please.' Wesley nodded, and the teacher turned back to her board.

Wesley reached into his backpack. He tried to find a new one. He pulled one from out of the sack. He looked back to the light. When he did so, The Eyes seemed to fade away slowly. As they did so, Wesley heard a strange phrase said to him. 'You'll see me again, boy.'

Then, it came. At the very moment, The Eyes vanished from view, and the school bell rang out. Ms. Ezequiel allowed the class to be dismissed. Everyone naturally stood up from their seats: Except for three people. Wesley leapt from his seat. He took off out of the class as fast as his legs would allow him. Gemma leaped up. She gave chase after him. Ms. Ezequiel had no idea what she had seen as both kids rushed past the front desk. Alec, on the other hand, remained in his seat. 'Lucky boy,' he snorted.

Devon kept on running up and down the halls. Gemma was hot on his tail as he ran through corridor after corridor to getaway. With every stride, he could feel the little tart snapping at his heels and breathing down his neck. 'I guess additional PE does pay off in the end.' He made an incredibly sad joke in this situation. 'I wonder how David Beckham deals with this in real life.' He raced up the stairs at lightning speed. He ran through the historic halls, almost knocking a supply teacher off his feet. The end of the staircase laid dead ahead. Wesley was about to take the stairs when a large object collapsed down the stairwell. It caught Wesley off guard. He stopped dead in his tracks. He rushed to see where the object landed. But, there was nothing to see. Gemma tried to stop as well when she saw he had stayed still. But it was too late. She smacked into him from behind and fell down the stairwell Wesley was looking into. She hit the ground with a massive thud.

There was a gasp of horror when she splattered onto the floor. People rushed to see what had happened and tried to help. Wesley ran up to the higher floors to see who had dropped the object. There didn't seem to be anyone around there. Wesley felt nervous and very guilty. Not wanting to be implicated in anyway with the accident, he obeyed his strong impulse to walk away from the scene. No one could see him. An ambulance was called, and Gemma was taken away. The stairwell was roped off to ensure no one could fall through.

The Sleepover

Friday. This was the night of the annual end of year school sleepover. All of the students in attendance arrived at the school at 7 PM. Inside the building, it was full of cool snacks. There was a couple of staff on hand to greet them. They would be staying through the night on hand to look after the students. The night had been fun throughout. Very soon, it was time for the guys to go to bed.

Wesley placed his sleeping bag next to both Alec and Jade. He laid down quietly in the same pyjamas he was wearing when his dad found him watching the horror film. There he was, staring at the ceiling in silence. Jade next door gave him a poke on his right shoulder. Wesley reacted and turned his neck towards her.

'What's the matter?' Wesley asked.

Jade plucked up enough courage to make her question known. 'You don't seriously believe that the story about a devil student is true, do you?' She murmured silently.

Wesley was none the wiser for this matter. He rubbed his eyes clear. 'I wish I could know for sure,' he sighed regretfully. 'I suppose you could say that it is for you to decide for yourself.'

Jade contemplated this. 'Yes, but did you not see The Eyes for yourself? You must know that they are out there'. She added more to her deduction. 'Why are you still here and alive if you have seen them? Alec said that many people had not survived their encounters'.

'How the hell should I know?' Wesley snorted. 'I guess I am just a lucky guy. But that isn't enough, really'. He rolled over on the pillow. He felt there was something wrong with life. Lots of things were hard for him now.

Alec had been listening to them for a while. He piped up as well. 'Can you keep the conversations down to a minimum please, you noisy wrecks?' He said crossly.

'Try telling that to the troublemakers in the years below us,' Wesley contradicted. 'You have no idea what our lives are like now. Just think how far we have come since back in 2010'.

'He does have a point,' Jade observed. 'We were all like that back then—even you, dude. We've grown, lost, changed, developed, etc.'.

'And besides, those brats can be handled,' Wesley waged. 'I have the strength and a commanding edge. You forget I was council rep for Year 9'.

'You weren't particularly good at it,' Alec reminded. 'It was good you left when you did. You would have been in a world of shit'.

There was a small laugh as Caitlynn arrived. She was wearing a nightie with no shoes, her red toenails showing. The red colour looked radiant. She had a very abrupt opinion. 'I actually can't wait for the end of school,' she observed. 'Counting down the days until we get to go away.'

'Onto bigger, better and much brighter things indeed,' Alec agreed. 'But, let's not forget the awesome memories we had here.'

'That's absolutely true, sir,' Wesley agreed. 'One of my favourites was when there was a Star Wars day here. I dressed up as Kylo Ren, and you Alec dressed as Darth Vader. You messed up your face with the burnt makeup. Man, you gave Mrs. James a scare. I thought she was going to go pale as well.'

'Well, she should not have asked me to take off the mask.' Alec protested.

'Consider yourself lucky, no one called a hospital.' Jade warned.

Everyone had fun for a good time before they all fell right off to sleep.

The wind was blowing outside the school. This was a breeze that had not been around for a good while. It felt very cool outside against the window and through the school hall. The blinds made a creaky sound against the speed of the wind. Wesley tilted his head front and back against the noise. It sounded whiny in his ear. He eventually gave up on trying to deal with it. He smacked his hands against the sleeping bag. He noticed the window was open at the middle-end of the massive hall.

'Probably best if I go up and close that window.' He whispered silently to himself. He stood up slowly and quietly as not to disturb anyone around him. He rose out of the sleeping bag and stood away from it onto the cold floor tiles. He walked towards the open window. As he did so, the howling of the wind got louder and louder with every step. He reached out for the lever that closed the window tight. As he began to pull it down, the face of the blind child, Phil crossed his. His dull expression on his face was fierce and grim. He was holding his cane in his hand and facing Wesley. The boy's heart skipped a beat over to the next one. He could tell shit was about to go down. He knew Phil was in the room when he was being touched inappropriately. He felt it would be time to face the music about what was going on: Especially with his involvement in Gemma's accident.

'The girl is in plaster you should know,' Phil noted. 'She should be out of the hospital in the next week. No thanks to you'.

'That wasn't my fault,' Wesley said. 'She came after me. There were things going on around me'.

'Just one excuse after another,' Phil wrote off his statements. 'You were there, and you mark as a deadly cause. You know that she could die if things get ugly. The blood will be on your hands'.

'What's got into you?' Wesley shuddered.

Phil ignored this question and focused on something else. 'You are an unfit human,' he snarled. 'The Eyes must exist. They will enthral this school with all their evil. You will see it become a legion of Hell before you join it'.

'What are you talking about?' Wesley gasped for breath. He was still quite alarmed by being surprised. 'Why are you doing this? You cannot destroy this place. The Eyes have no power over us all'.

'Yes, they have. You just don't see it yet.'

'They will never destroy us,' Wesley snapped back. 'Never.'

Phil snarled and growled at the boy's futile words. He inched closer to the glass. He placed his palm on the window.

'You have no words to destroy us, boy,' he said. 'The Eyes have more power in them than you can imagine. They will come for you in the death of night.

You will discover this tonight. That is my promise'.

And with that, Phil slunk away. Wesley was so shocked; he slammed the window shut and ran back to the bed.

The Small Hours

The time passed quickly. It was now three o'clock. The moon was still up. It was still dark out with hardly any light being shone. Wesley had been dosing silently. He had not stirred at all since he had shut the window. He next woke up an hour later. He sat and felt something was wrong. He placed a hand on his forehead. He felt moisture cover it. It smelt fowl to his nostrils. The same moisture was also on his chin and the rest of his neck. It felt oily and grubby. It appeared he had been sweating in the night. This shouldn't have been the case, for it did not make a heap of sense. The heating had been low during the night, and the window was shut. Wesley was aware of how hot it had been this summer. But, this was way too abnormal for this night and situation.

Wesley got up out of his sleeping bag. He felt around the area looking out for anything tangible. He reached out and clasped his torch and his mobile telephone. He made his way to the double doors at the end of the massive assembly hall. He pushed through them with his brutish force and made his way into the school canteen.

Once inside the canteen, it was pitch black. The dark was thick and all-consuming. It looked like nothing was there at all. Devon shook the flashlight he was carrying and turned it on. He altered the brightness of the light and cast it all around the eating area. Confident he could see in the dark, he made more of a movement to walk on. In the light he produced, he could see everything clearly, even if the torchlight were limited to a circle. He could see the table, chairs, and water fountains. At least he knew where he was walking.

'Jesus Christ,' He whispered. 'When did this school get so scary this week? It's like living in the movie IT. There are so many horrors lurking in the shadows and the dark. Lucky us, we're all in it. Some ideas to have this sleepover. Why is all of this here? What did we do to deserve a haunting like this? What did I do?' Wesley felt very awkward, talking to himself in the dark. But, was he alone?

'Why don't you do me the honour of asking me yourself?' There was a deadly voice from somewhere around the large eating arena. Wesley felt the voice vibrate against his ear. He turned around to see The Eyes open up. They zoomed in towards him and charged. Wesley shuddered as if he had never seen them before. 'Huh? No. No. No. AAAAAAAAAAAAAAAAAAARRRRRRRRRRRRRRR RRRRRRRRRRGGGGGGGGGGGGGGGGGGGGGGGG GGGHHHHHHHHHHHHHHHHHHHHHHHH!!!'

Wesley had never screamed so loud in his life. The Eyes gave chase towards him. They blazed at the smell of fear and blood. They lunged for him. Wesley knew he must run for it as fast as possible. As he did so, the beat of his slippers caused a rippling sound around the school premises.

Wesley ran as fast as he could. He could feel the speed of The Eyes beating down on him as he passed through the kitchen and the hall. Alec, Jade and the rest of the girls had moved spots during the night and were now located in one of the maths rooms. They had heard Wesley scream out loud. Alec peered around the edge of the door to see him running towards the room at his top speed.

'Mate! Wesley! Wes!' Alec gasped, trying to keep awake from his untimely awakening. 'What the hell is going on here? Don't you know what time it is?' There was nothing much else he could do except gasp for breath. Wesley shot through yelling at the top of his voice. 'Don't just stand there, you big-headed fool!' He was screaming so loud he didn't care for what he was saying. 'Run for YOUR LIVES!' He yelled as he sped by. 'IT'S THE EYES! THE EYES! THEY'RE HERE!'

The students were in great disbelief. 'What the bloody hell are you talking about?' Jade asked. She peered around as well. Enough for her lilac coloured pyjama bottoms and gold pyjama top to be visible. They all turned their heads and came out of the room. They could all see the floating orange objects of death. But, this also meant they could be seen by them too. Alec had no idea what to think of this sighting.

'That's not possible!' He exclaimed. 'You were a story. And a legend. I never thought you happened'.

'I did happen,' The Eyes spoke in their deep horrific tone. 'Every story you hear happens whether you believe it or not. And I am a perfectly accurate one of that description'.

Hailey was not satisfied with this tone. She emerged from the group. She was wearing a furry onesie. 'You are a sick bastard. You destroyed my sister mentally. You sent my dad on a wild goose chase. You made a fool out of us all'. She was furious in her berating. 'You are going to pay tenfold for the mental agony we have suffered.'

'What can a child like you do to a creature like me?' The Eyes hissed.

'You will kindly come forward into the light this moment. You will unveil yourself before us'. Hailey held her moral ground in front of pure evil. She wanted to know the truth of this thing'.

'You only had to ask, my dear,' The Eyes agreed to these demands. Graciously, The Eyes had accepted. They began to come slowly forward into the sight range of the teenagers. The team was quite nervous about the being before them. 'Something tells me that we should back up a little bit.' One of them tugged on Hailey's arm in warning.

'Be quiet, Caitlynn!' Hailey said. 'I am confronting this thing whether anyone likes it or not.'

Hailey firmly held his head high as The Eyes came even closer.

Then, it happened. Just as The Eyes were within an inch of Hailey's face, there came a massive crack over The Eyes. They collapsed to the floor. There then was a loud horrifying scream of pain. A small spot of blood suddenly appeared on the floor. The Eyes had to be a solid person. The scream of pain then turned into a cry of sorrow. 'Someone put a light on for the love of God,' Alec said. Jade did so and flicked a switch on the wall. The light came on to show rows of rooms. There was also a grim sight.

There was Wesley Devon, standing with great power, over a poor Phil Bridges, exhaling strangely. In his hand was a piece of shaved-down PE equipment. The young lad had smacked Phil over the head with a rounder's sports bat. The team had never seen such a display of violence. The massive impact had left Phil with a nasty gash over his forehead. The nasty cut was bleeding down his face. It looked excruciating. Such a violent attack as worthy of great reactions.

Caitlynn Missin was so enraged at such an assault. She wrestled the bat away from Wesley as he was left shocked to the bone as to what he had just done. 'Wesley Devon, you stupid son of a bitch!' She scolded crossly. 'What the hell is wrong with you, you sick douche? How could you do such a thing? Beating Phil."

'You could've killed him,' Jade added, joining in on the act.

Wesley had no idea how to respond. He tried to make a run for it. Alec caught and held him where he was. 'You're not going anywhere. Kindly explain yourself, you little shit'.

Devon tried to get a word in with the people who were turning against him. He looked towards Phil, whom he was sure had left the school building after his taunts. 'It's him, guys. He is the one who is behind all of this. You gotta hear me out over this. He's the reason why Gemma has ended up in the hospital. He is the main link with The Devil Student'.

'You've still smacked him over the bloody head, you prick'.

None of Wesley's friends would accept his self-defence argument. It seemed like he was trapped in his actions. Alec starred down him in great disgust at the visual evidence. 'Of all the dumbest stuff I have heard, Wesley,' he said. 'That has to be the largest pile of horse muck I have ever heard in my life'. He held strong denial. Wesley was shocked his best friend would not show him support. It would also appear that Hailey agreed with those siding against him. 'You would say anything to make yourself top boy. That's how you won your election. You are all mouth and no trousers. If I didn't know any better, I would say this was all because of you'.

Wesley felt appalled at what was being suggested of him. There was more to this, in his opinion. 'The Eyes are coming for me just as much as they for you. Just as much as they for your sister and your father,' He protested. 'Gemma is in the hospital because of what The Eyes made her do. Now all of us are exposed to them by default. Don't you guys understand?'.

None of the teens had any idea what to believe. No idea what to believe in the story. They still had a conviction that Wesley was involved in the actions. They then, against the will of the accused child, picked Phil up off the floor, patched him up and got him on his way. Both Phil and Wesley kept their eyes on each other as the rest of the day was about to begin. Wesley was starting to feel like the powers of The Eyes were in motion.

Death

Consequences. All of our actions have them. The weekend's time passed by as if it meant nothing. The Monday school day played with its natural self. Wesley's actions toward Phil had caused him a great deal of trouble. The headmaster, Mr. Wilson, had called him into his office that break time for an extreme disciplinary meeting. Wesley sat in the small chair facing his armchair. He felt like he was being questioned for a crime: Of course, assault is a significant criminal offense. And, when Mr. Wilson had heard what had happened on the night in question, he was not happy in the slightest.

'Wesley Samuel Devon, I am thoroughly ashamed of you,' he raged ferociously at the Year 11 student. 'Where in the name of God would you get off attacking a student less fortunate than yourself. What do you have to say for yourself? You had better have a good explanation for what you have done, boy'.

Wesley tried to defend his ground over such a disastrous situation. He felt deeply sorry for what he had done to Phil. But, he still wanted to put the case forward for The Eyes.

'I'm waiting!' Mr. Wilson folded his arms as he patiently waited for an answer.

'Sir, I must protest,' Wesley finally spoke through a stomach of guilt. 'The boy Philip Bridges is something dangerous. There is something wrong with that boy. You know what I am talking about. Can you not see this with your own eyes, sir?' He asked.

'As a matter of fact, I can,' Mr. Wilson growled. 'There is a nasty cut that you put across his face with a cricket bat.'

'It was a rounders bat,' Wesley muttered.

'I beg your pardon,' Wilson hissed. He sensed a tone of sassiness.

'N-N-N-Nothing' Wesley stuttered.

'That's what I thought you said, Devon,' the Headmaster assumed. 'Never answer back to me again.'

Wesley Devon felt very foolish for his choice of actions and words in front of a person of power.

'You have no idea how much trouble you could be in, young man,' Mr. Wilson said. 'if that blow to the head had killed Phil, you would for sure be expelled without a chance of reprieve and facing charges of murder. Think about that, boy'.

Wesley gulped at such a comment. He imagined what it would mean if he were expelled and put in prison. He would never live with the shame. His parents would be super mad at him. He would not have a friend in the world. He would not be able to enter polite society for the rest of his life. He hung his head in remorse.

'However,' Mr. Wilson added. 'You have a surprising lifeline. This term has only one more week left of it. And to expel a Year 11 at this stage is a pointless attribute. So, for the rest of this term, you will spend it in the isolation room, days on end. We will only allow you to come out for break and lunchtime and the end of term celebrations'.

'Isn't the Isolation Room burnt down?' Wesley commented again.

'The condition of that room is of no concern to me,' Mr. Wilson retorted. 'And, if you value leaving this school with any qualifications, you would make it sure that its condition means nothing to you.'

Wesley felt himself to be told straight and clear.

Mr. Wilson had declared his sentence firmly. Then he proceeded to dismiss him. 'Now, if you are satisfied enough with this, I would suggest that you pick up your bag off the coffee table and get out of my sight. Before I change my mind and reach for the expulsion paperwork'.

The guilty boy hung his head for a second time at that meeting. He picked up his bag and headed out of the door into the creepy hallway. The Headmaster's office was at the far end of a corridor with several framed pictures glaring down on him. Vincent sealed the door and locked himself into his office. 'The nerve of some people,' he scoffed as he returned to the desk. He set up to type at his computer to input the isolation record for Wesley Devon. Once he was satisfied, it was complete, he leaned back in his chair to sip a cup of coffee. He had never been so angry in his life. He had been used to this with Year 7's. But, not Year 11's.

Little did the strict Headmaster know was that by closing the door, he had sealed his fate. As soon as he was leaning back in his chair in comfort, he caught sight of them: The Eyes. They were blazing with fury and anger. They felt the fear of the powerful head.

'No.' Vincent coughed up a shock. 'This cannot be. You're them?'

The Eyes loomed and hovered like a balloon towards the frightened man. Their devilish glow intensified and strengthened beyond the heat of an oven. Wilson screamed a terrible scream that could be heard for miles. He screamed his last as his life was wiped clean out of him in the blink of one of The Eyes. They then faded with an evil villainous laugh.

Mrs. James and Ms. Ezequiel were nearby in the office when they heard the scream. Wesley hadn't gone far away when he too heard what was yelled. He raced back to the office to see what the commotion was. He and the two members of staff tried to force down the door. But, by the time they had done so and breached it wide, it was already too late. Vincent laid on the floor with a pale face. He looked as if he had been choked to death with a thick cord of rope.

'You ought to check a pulse,' Mrs. James advised. Ms. Ezequiel inched down as close as she could get and held her two first fingers to his neck. She couldn't feel anything. 'I got nothing,' she denied. 'Yeah, he's dead. Nothing there'.

'How could this happen?' Wesley asked in shock. He looked at the computer. Without a signature on the isolation document, it had incredibly become null and void. In some extent, he had escaped the school justice.

'Who knows?' Mr. Ezequiel pondered. 'I think we have foul play going on around this place.'

The staff wasn't sure. One thing was certain though: There'd be extraordinarily little sleep for them that night.

Emergency Meeting

The news of the headmaster's death reached far across the area. People were in awe of the circumstances. The student's reactions were decidedly mixed. They began hearing different stories of the cause. The most common story they had heard for this was that Mr. Wilson had killed himself. The students were not sure what to believe about his passing, and the mysterious goings-on related to The Eyes. A lot of them gathered around a large table after school to discuss information.

'Suicide?' Alec reacted with strong scepticism at the rumour. 'Is that what they are putting this down to? That cannot be right!'

'I'm afraid that is the way it looks,' Wesley reported. 'At least I won't be locked up in the Isolation Room.'

'Stay focused, dude,' Jade reminded.

'I'm sorry, I gotta call bullshit on this,' Hailey piped up. 'Wilson would not just kill himself at a time like this. It would not make sense for how the year has been built up. The only thing I could think of it is murder'.

Wesley made a confused face. 'That's more of a stretch to suicide. But, how could he have been killed if he was the only person in that room when I left it?' He asked.

Regretfully, there was not a definite answer as to how this death came about. The fact he was alone in his office when it happened only made the theorising even more difficult. Now, no one was entirely sure about what meant what with who.

'Those Eyes of The Devil Student are fearful and as dangerous as the stories make them out to be,' Becca pondered as she sat down next to her sister. 'Striking as if it means nothing. No wonder no one knew who he was or what he looked like'.

It was this interesting comment that made Wesley put on a thoughtful face. A few conundrums began to form in his mind.

'What is it, bruv?' Alec asked.

'A few thoughts have occurred to me.' Wesley said as he began to speak his mind out loud. 'Alec, do you remember saying that no one knew who, or what for that matter, The Devil Student is?' He asked.

'Yes, I do remember saying that,' Alec agreed. 'What of it?'

'I have just come up with something,' Wesley said.

'Go on, we're all listening,' Caitlynn accepted.

'My theory is that Phil is one person who knows who The Devil Student is. He knows something about this mess. And it's not something he can tell because it betrays the idea it's even a person at all. Therefore, he is in league with The Eyes. Mainly so they can destroy all knowledge of The Eyes from the neighbourhood. The question is as to what end?'

'That would imply that he wants to destroy us in the process,' Hailey began to guess a few more connections. 'That would explain a lot about my sister's and my dad's ordeal.'

Becca nodded, confirming what was being considered. But, she too had things to add to this convoluted debate. 'There's still a bit more. Mr. Wilson rejected the story. I might think The Eyes killed him out of anger/retaliation. Gemma didn't know anything about The Eyes'.

'That could've been an accident,' Alec argued.

'It was,' Wesley muttered. He still found it hard to talk about what happened on the stairs.

Becca continued further. 'And don't forget the fact I only heard about this stuff from eavesdropping on the story. The next thing, I have nightmares, and people think I'm crazy. The point is, we've all be affected in some way and made to do terrible things'.

'True, true,' Jade nodded. 'So, we're all connected by these things by things we've done. None of this seems to make any lick of sense. What is the full connection?'

After she asked this question, the lights began to buzz. Wesley knew that The Eyes were upon them for sure.

Wesley got up in shock as The Eyes appeared above all of the group.

'Oh shit,' Wesley gasped.

'Why don't you take the time to ask me yourself?' The Eyes offered as the floated in towards them all. Everyone dived for cover. 'I have been waiting for you all to be here. Now is the time I take revenge on those who know of my terrors. YOU'RE MINE NOW FOREVER!'.

Everyone took off and ran in different directions at the same time. It was a large full-scale chase. Wesley tried to keep up with all of the teens. But, he was not fast enough. He dived off down a hallway past the reception area. He ran through the halls as fast as he could. But, it was tiring easy. The Eyes were catching up to him. Wesley dived along the longest corridor by far until he reached the lower reception area. The last door to it opened up. The bad news was that he completely cut off from the rest of the school. He looked around the small area he was now in. He looked like he was on his own. But, it would not remain this way.

Everyone else, they had run fast. They looked to see that The Eyes were nowhere to be seen. But, they could also see that Wesley was nowhere to be seen. Alec looked around. No signs. The only thing there was to deduce was that he was now in grave danger. He raced to get back into the school and reach Wesley in time.

Wesley, at this point, was making his ways through the curving halls. There was so much suspense crawling across the premises. The shadows on the walls loomed over Wesley like branches on a tree. It was as if his heart was going to fall out of his chest and land right in front of him. Then, there was trouble. A dead-end appeared right in front of him and cut off his escape.

'There's nowhere left for me to run,' he panicked in a calm voice. He felt his back sweat a river. The Eyes had caught up to him and were now upon him like sand on a yellow beach. He turned around to see them looking at him on his level. He glared at them, hiding every ounce of fear he had tucked in his mind. The Eyes morphed around him and transported him to the bottom of the staircase where Gemma came crashing down. He knew there was nowhere he could run where The Eyes could find him. It seemed he was screwed. He was caught up, pinned by The Eyes.

'I guess this is where it all comes down,' Wesley observed. 'Phil knows about you. You come here to us at the end of tenure. For some reason, I am important to you. Yet, with every turn of the page, there's one more mystery after another. I just don't get it.'

The Eyes made a communicative statement. 'You would find that throughout life that there are many things that cannot be explained.'

Wesley was not satisfied with this comment. 'What am I supposed to gain from all of this mayhem? Who are you because no one knows who you are?'

The Eyes fell silent like the cold wind. Wesley felt very ignored by this supernatural being. 'Well. Are you not going to answer me? Who is he in the story of the Devil Student?'.

The Eyes responded emotionlessly with a corrective statement about its true identity.

'I am not a he,' came the chilling voice of death. 'As an entity, I can be anything I want to be. I have manifested myself through what people have seen, where they have been, and by what they find out from the legends. Furthermore on my origin, I was never a boy. I am far more than you imagine, Wesley. I am a very part of yourself'.

Wesley was alarmed at this. 'What the hell does that mean?' The fearful lad asked the being. 'You cannot just be a pair of Eyes. What are you? Come into the light and show yourself in your real form'.

The Eyes snarled. 'You only had to ask.' The Eyes twitched. They were slowly changing shape. Starting from The Eyes and morphing out to the outline of a body. Wesley watched in amazement as the body was revealed to be of a girl's figure. The shape of a little girl: No taller than what he was. But, he felt that the age was wrong for her; Older than he was, maybe so. Her figure was obscure, but not unrecognisable. She was Year 10 in appearance. Her hair was short: Bob length. Blonde in contrast to Wesley's chocolate brown shade. She was clothed in ordinary, casual clothes. Her t-shirt was purple with blue stripes.

Her thighs were left exposed, yet she was wearing a skirt coloured in black and white designs resembling fear. The changing yellow light brought them to pigmentation and emphasised her lower half. Her feet were bare. Her toes were grubby. Her clothes were ripped and torn apart at the ends. They resembled the kind of marks attained after being burnt. The blood was visible all over her body in different parts. Wesley felt amazed at what he was bearing witness to. The girl stood up to the boy and opened her newly visible mouth. The phrase that came out amazed Wesley in all ways.

'Hello, brother,' she uttered in the creepiest tone possible.

Wesley was not expecting such an introduction. His lips quivered as he tried to respond to her. 'B…B…B…B…Brother?' He finally managed to say out loud. The girl cracked her neck and spoke of her nature.

'Yes. Indeed. I am your sister, and you are my younger brother. Your parents never told you about me. Did they?'

Wesley did not recall such a conversation ever having taken place. He had always known his family was hiding something. He was beginning to think this was the hidden secret. He began to think and wanted to know more from these stories.

'Who are you? Can you at least tell me what your name is?' Wesley asked.

The girl agreed to speak her identity. 'My name is Molly. Molly Chloe Devon. I was born long before you were. It was 14 years, to be exact. Your mother, our mother was a 16-year-old. Kicked out onto the streets of London by her strict Catholic parents. Contact cut off. Hence why you never met your grandparents. To mother, you had none.

Although, I must confess we're not full blood. We do not share the same parents. You were born of a mother with a dad's loving hand to take your tiny body into the world. I, on the other hand, I am born of your blood, and Satan himself'.

'The Devil Student,' Wesley had seemed to piece everything together fully. 'We cannot be related to that. You cannot be serious'.

The other student friends of Wesley began to regroup and joined out of sight of the spirited girl. They kept their own eyes on Wesley as he was spoken to by the creature. They could see Wesley had nowhere to go. They would not be prepared for what was to happen.

'You killed Mr. Wilson. You bashed up Gemma. You terrorised the Southerland sister,' Wesley recalled.

'People you do not like, Both Wilson and Gemma. The Southerland sisters do not care for you. They blamed you for what happened to them and the heartlet,' Molly taunted, meanly.

'That's not true. You are lying. You have been lying the whole time,' Wesley denied as the other students joined beside him. They had no idea what they were looking at.

'The deaths are true. If I had my way more, everyone I met or who were foolish to come up against me would never be alive to tell the tale'.

'You couldn't destroy me. You wouldn't do it. You kept following me constantly over the week'.

'I was trying to find you. And I did. I have always been there. Day after day, trying to reach out. I sat there, invisible in that lonely chair at the dinner table.

Nothing would suffice. I created civil unrest across this school for you to enjoy as a match to destroy all that is good. I never cared for right and wrong; neither should you. That is why you were looked down on in this cruel neighbourhood. By making you beat the blind brat, I set the stones for your transformation to pure evil powers'.

'Enough of this,' Wesley snapped. 'I don't care about that. I want a family. I don't have one at all. Why would I care for that kind of power when there is no one to share it with? Can you answer that, Molly Chloe Devon?'

Alec emerged from the back. 'So, you are the woman behind The Eyes. How come it was that no one knew your name or your basic identity?'

Molly described her shallow life while she was alive. 'I chose that I should keep myself to myself. No one there would respect it at all. Or what I did you show that I no longer want this school in my life. I have a right to be by myself and live my life as I want'.

'No one said otherwise. But you did not have to be like the way you were'. Wesley held his ground and came in as close as he could: This was to become his biggest mistake in the conversation.

'I had every right to act as I did. You didn't respect me, and you paid through the nose. And now, I will make you all understand the truth: one way or another. You shall now see how powerful I can be to you'.

To prove her evil point, she reached out and grabbed hold of Wesley's arm. Wesley yelped out in pain as the spirit's arm squeezed onto the bone. Dark magic began to coil from her arm to his and seep into his skin, like a disease on the sick. Hailey tried to rush forward to help him. Alec held her back. There was nothing they could do to help the boy. Wesley looked at himself in horror as dark clouds of evil magic covered him.

Wesley's skin began to turn to a tanned glow: Just like his phantom sister. Fire was spilling out and suffocating the boy. He felt himself change and get even hotter and stranger.

'What are you doing?' Alec gasped.

To which the girl referred to as 'POSSESSION!'

Wesley's friends cowered at the sight of the girl of The Eyes forcing their evil energy into the eyes of her brother. It was such a hideous transformation for the young boy. His breath suddenly began to lessen and lessen as the evil Devil Student fused herself with him. It looked chilling and very absorbing for the boy to experience. In turn, Wesley's eyes turned to a fiery hot red. They resembled the colour of the fabled Eyes of the story. His face then contorted to a sinful hideous creature. He felt his face itch and change drastically. His chin got larger, and skin became rawer and disfigured.

Alec was livid as to what he was watching. And furious as well.

'What the heck is wrong with you, you sick bitch?' He lambasted the creature as she turned her brother to an evil being. 'What did you do to him, you monster?' He demanded roughly.

The Devilish child explained herself to the confident boy. 'Don't you see, Hanks? As newly full siblings due to my enhancement, Wesley and I will rule God's earth and turn it into a hell he would fear. We will take back this planet and form it how it should be'.

'No, you won't,' Alec defied. 'You have no means to do that. Let him go. Let go of him'.

'I will do no such thing,' Molly refused to obey this command: Like all the rules she never obeyed in life. Sure enough, her powers were now fully latched onto her only living brother. Soon, the good kind boy in him was to be quashed by the evil of his sister. He looked like a full embodiment of evil. Hailey strongly began to panic as she tried to reason with the trapped boy's soul.

'Wesley, listen to me,' she said. 'Please! You can fight this. My family cares about you. And we want you in our lives. You need to fight this thing. You are far stronger than her and far stronger than you believe you are'.

Molly's spirit laughed at such a pathetic attempt to revive her loved one. Hailey took great resentment from this. She went to strike her across the face. Just as she could bring a rough palm across her face, however, another arm caught it and held it tight.

'What point would there be in slapping this woman? It would be like touching a cloud,' Phil said as he walked into view of everyone. Although he had to tap out the floor with his special cane, he was aware of where he was standing and the situation around himself. 'Do not bother trying to interfere. This is the price you pay. There is nothing you can do to save him. Nor save yourselves'.

'Why are you involved in this?' Becca asked.

'I see how this world needs to be taught a lesson in how evil is stronger. It should be allowed to take its chance of ruling,' Phil justified. 'The Eyes reached out to me. I am a tool to help them conquer this futile world'.

'Wesley, are you hearing this?' Caitlynn screamed at the devil-turned boy. 'You need to hear this.'

'He cannot hear you, child,' Molly growled. 'He is mine to command, and my orders are the only ones he will follow.'

'Oh, you have crossed the line, you little son of a bitch,' Alec had never been so angered in his life. He charged forward. The devil student morphed in and out to avoid his foolish runs up. All the time, she refused to answer his futile questions and comments. The young lad then saw the right to make a fist and throw it forward for a punch. His fist was within inches of the ghostly creature's face when a strong supernatural arm held it back from her. Alec tried to budge over and break free.

Alec looked up to see that the large arm belonged to the boy, Wesley. He was distraught and in a lot of trouble. He could see the visible damages to his face. It had been contorted with signs of infection and disease. Boils and scars. It was not a pretty sight to look at.

'GET OFF ME!' Alec barked loudly, and he tried to wriggle free. There was no way he could not be scared or not look at Wesley's damaged face. He looked as if he was the casualty of a house fire and had only escaped. Wesley then spoke down to the foolish child. When he did speak, his voice has morphed to several lower octaves. He sounded almost like Darth Vader. It was just as chilling to hear up close.

'You are a puny human being. To think you can just attack a delicate spirit,' he said. 'You have no right to lay hands on my sister,' he boomed loudly to the boy his age. 'She belongs to me, and no one else. She is her being. No one else's. Nor can she be beaten up by an immature fool like yourself'.

'He's under her spell. That's not him talking,' Hailey observed.

'That's bloody obvious, I can see,' Alec said in a fit of panic. He then felt himself not touching the floor as Wesley picked him up off the floor. The strength gained from the possession was impossible to calculate as Alec rose above the ground. He then found himself to be thrown over to the other side of the stairway. He felt himself crash into the wall with a great thud. Caitlynn rushed to his side to see if he had broken anything. Luckily, there were no such breaks.

'Are you ok?' She asked blindly as she arrived.

'Never mind about this,' Alec coughed loudly as Wesley advanced in his direction. 'RUN!!!'

The group of teens made a break for it as Wesley began to make chase at them. They had to run back the way they came. They back through the halls and out of the school: Not looking back. The Devil student and her blind servant morphed slowly around the possessed Wesley Devon. They held hands in a circle.

'Our linking of the union is complete,' Molly declared in evil glee. 'The world will soon see how strong evil is. The world will be dissolved in flames and fires of hell. It will then be remade over in our glory. Only evil will exist. The valuable practises of Lucifer will be honoured and upheld'.

The gents began to laugh evilly and creepily. Hell was going to break lose all over the world.

'And, if any of God's human beings, loyal to the will of good, dare try to rise against our powers, try to defy the will of the higher powers, shall be put in their rightful places, be forced to answer to The Deathless Prince himself, and be turned to evil and live as slaves to him for the rest of their miserable lives.'

Meanwhile, the team had run as far as away from the school as they could get. It was a massive stroke of luck that they had made it out at all. They breathed a heavy sigh of relief together. It was impossible not to notice an obvious blank that Wesley was not there and that he had been taken away by the creature's powers. They darted slowly into Alec's house at the end of the road. Alec bolted the door and made sure it was secure: So that no one could burst through and attack them. None of them had any idea of what they had just seen. Hailey was not happy with the owner of the house.

'You just laid there, cowering,' she scolded. 'You didn't even try to break Wesley away from the bitch.'

'There was nothing I could have done to save him,' Alec denied sadly. 'That thing had enough strength to take me over just as much as it took Wes.'

'Yeah, but now what are we going to do?' Hailey asked. 'Now we have two issues to attend to. Destroy that thing and get them back. But how would we do it?'

'I dare not think it,' Jade thought. 'But, somehow, we have to take her down and do away with Phil. He's her only link to the outside world. Cut that off, and you cut off her chances of knowing of us.'

'But, if we tried to take down anything that helps her, it could cost us, Wesley,' Alec considered. 'Either way, the villain wins hands down.'

As on many occasions, the group had many different ideas to think of. Yet, they all seemed to fall flat of any conviction. Caitlynn thought of something else. 'Perhaps you kill that being as if she was some kind of vampire,' she bravely suggested. 'You know what I mean, steaks crosses and cutting off their ugly head.'

'You watch way too many classic films,' Becca insinuated.

'No, more of Twilight,' Caitlynn denied.

Becca tried to hide her disappointment falsely.

Amongst this foolish talk of a mediocre film, Alec had been thinking of more. He had nodded in agreement. 'There's a lot of truth in this. And it could be done. But, as with everything, there's always a cost. You actually could not kill The Eyes without killing our boy'.

Everyone realised that The Devil Student and Phil were far cleverer than them: Even smarter to use every conundrum against them. What could they do? There was no way to have the good without the bad.

The Next Tragedy

The day passed; People had noticed that a lot had changed. They were aware that some people were not around the school. But, few dared to ask the causes. Lessons fell deadly silent. Break times felt less fun with the socialising. The remaining members of the group kept each other safe around the playground. Hailey's phone rang at lunchtime. She answered it. A long conversation followed down the line until she put the phone down with a long sigh.

'What happened?' Caitlynn asked, becoming suspicious. 'Who was that you were talking to?'

Hailey turned across to her friend and whispered that it was an older sibling of a friend they knew.

Jade was intrigued that someone obscure had her number. Not wanting to draw attention to this, she changed the subject, and she asked: 'What did they say?'

'It's Gemma. She's dead,' was the answer that none of them wanted to hear.

The group was aghast at what they had heard. They had never heard anything so shocking before. They thought it was a tragic outcome to occur for a girl her age. The team wondered what must have been going through the minds of her family.

'Dead?' Alec finally gasped for speech. 'How do you mean? Was it the fall that did her in?'

'Pretty much,' Hailey observed as cold as ice. 'She fell a great depth and at a massive speed. All for chasing Wesley. A boy she didn't even love. The impact of the fall left her in a deathlike coma from which she would never wake up'.

'Hence dead,' Jade sighed. 'Such a twisted end to a girl like her.'

The group of survivors felt very forlorn with what had occurred. Death is never an easy subject, regardless of any time. There would be more blood on their hands if Molly weren't stopped.

'How on Earth are we ever going to explain this to the rest of the school? They'll be more questions than we can answer,' Caitlynn wondered with great sadness.

No one had any logical idea of how to, or even wanted to tell anyone. But, it would not be that simple. It was only until the point where Alec finally spoke and declared: 'We need to take down this son of a bitch. And this time, she has to stay down in the dirt'.

As the young adolescent's had gathered, Gemma's family was in monumental tatters over the death of the girl. The girls visited their place of residence the following day to pay their respects and offer a great deal of comfort. Already, the team was going through so much at the benefit of The Eyes' reign of terror. Alec, on the other hand, tried to keep himself to himself without going over the edge. He carried on with his usual stuff and lessons that he did during the day.

How, indeed, could things be contained? It wasn't too long before the news of what had happened to poor Gemma Beckett to infect the whole school and spread into the street. The press was all geared for a field day, and now they had it. Lots of children's parents were incredibly enraged that something this tragic would happen to a girl of her 'popularity.' The responsibility of the children's safety was called into question. The staff had no idea what to think. A public enquiry was to be ordered against the school's misconduct. The future of the school's credibility depended on good hearings from the enquiry. Regretfully, without a strong living teaching staff member of Mr. Wilson's position, no legal or strong defence claim could be made in the school's honour. It was naturally one piece of bad luck after another.

Therefore, the head of the School Governors Board, Mr. Edward Hardy Griffin, was left with no choice but to close the school down until further notice. If things got any worse, it would likely be closed for good. Many futures were in danger of coming clattering down before the teens had even begun to live their lives.

The students were sent home with work to keep them tied over. This was good for their revision, yet they were strongly advised that they should prepare for the risk that the year's exams would not be finished. The staff felt the strains as well, many leading to mental breakdowns.

A thick, uncompromising cloud, black as the night, loomed over the whole school and the neighbourhood around it. The Assistant headteacher, now made an acting head due to his superior's demise, was most dismayed at the unfair, but non-negotiable, decision. He knew his role in the enquiry would be criticised by anyone he was known by. Nevertheless, no matter what he said, it did not affect the definite verdict on the closure. In terms of the criticism, many of the staff were dismayed at how things had played out: Specifically, Ms. Ezequiel. She had stern words with him in a local coffee shop on the corner of town. Mrs. James was with them too.

'What kind of head are you?' She snapped crossly. She smacked him on the chest with her leather gloves.

'I am not even headmaster at all. That man has been dead for a week. I am left here in his place. Left to pick up the pieces. What am I supposed to do? I only took notes at his side during meetings'.

'Did you not have any defiance in you, you dumb fool?' Ms. Ezequiel had never complained about anything like this in her life.

'I didn't know what to do in this situation,' George Goodman protested for his decisions or lack thereof. 'Even if there were a chance, they would have closed down the school no matter. What else could you expect?'. Mrs Ella James was not happy with this pathetic attitude. She rose from her stool and slapped the man across the cheek.

'You disgust me, George,' she raged. 'You are a weak-willed man. You are hardly fit to represent a school. It surprises me as to how you were picked as Vincent's deputy'.

Both women left him alone to reflect on what had been said to him. George felt very ridiculed for how he had behaved.

For all her faults and her reputation, the least that Gemma Ann Beckett deserved of herself was a decent send-off at her funeral. And so, when things had died down to a level of normality, the funeral was conducted in a churchyard. Her tearful family and the unopen school laid her to rest at her grave, just as had been done with the glorious headmaster. The day could not have looked anymore, gloomy.

During the sombre ceremony, some of the students took their seats towards the back of the church. It watched in silent sadness as the wooden coffin was lowered from view into the ground. The fresh soil against the hole was filled to the top. The poor girl was left to rest for one last time. Thick dark clouds loomed over the church cemetery.

Only Alec Hanks, of whom had now darkened dramatically due to the events of the past days, diverted his attention to the outside of the funeral area. He sceptically watched over to see the dark figure of a teen glare down on them with an ugly face. Alec began to stroll away from the graveyard after he had paid his long respects. He walked towards the edge of the street to meet up with the fearsome nosy persona. This person just so happened to be none other than Wesley Devon. His face looked like he had been out in the sun for too long. His once beautiful clear eyes had now been torched as red as sin. Powerfully, Alec stood face to face with him, not a glance of fear in his eyes as he spoke.

'This is as far as it goes,' Alec stated the grim facts. 'Two deaths and mental episodes are enough. And I meant that obvious, dude'. Wesley stared at him as blank as a clean whiteboard. 'This is where it all falls flat for everyone now,' Alec continued, daring a fierce reaction. 'You are as blameful in all of this horror as your dead sister is.'

Wesley remained as silent as the wind around them. He registered what was being said behind the berating's. Nevertheless, his haunting eye contact remained continually uninterrupted.

'Of course, you are a victim too,' Alec observed, balancing his opinions. 'Is there anything left of the old Wesley Devon inside there?' He chanced a glimmer of redemption. He scanned his ragged clothes up and down. He looked as his boiled face. 'Can you hear me, Wes? He must be somewhere. Maybe his mind pushed to the side by his sister. How else could The Eyes have a solid body to see us at work? What better host than a living relative? But, it cannot last'.

Wesley Devon remained ghostly silent. Hanks was feeling slightly awkward at this behaviour. 'Won't you at least say something, dude. You were happier enough to talk when you tried to snap my arm'.

Alec then felt a ghostly presence walk beside him with a dragging step. He turned to see it as Phil Bridges. 'Bide your time, son,' he said as he emerged. 'You have hardly any time left. Your tale will surely end when Molly has her way with this Earth. You'd better be getting back. They have some nice hors deVere's in the church. Soon, The Devil Student will come for you. She will come for all of you and send you to darker place than any hell created'.

Alec felt greatly confident that he would have rattled the minds of the two persons he stood with. 'I was going to guess you would say that, boy. I will also guess she won't be too far away. I'm in no hurry. She can come when she likes it. We will be ready for you when you come'.

And with that, Alec turned on his heels and sauntered away. He hid a private smile behind his back. But, if he looked back, he would've seen a small tear trickle down Wesley's cheek.

Parent's House

With the loss of two persons to grim ends, already, it seemed that there were little if no options left now. The students were now resorting to reconvening in the house of Wesley. Becca Southerland walked up to the home of the Devon's. The dad answered the door. Becca gulped as she tried to find the words to explain what had happened to his son. She finally gained her courage and spoke. The things she said were horrifying.

Nevertheless, Peter was happy to allow them into the house. He sensed a grave feeling of urgency. Regardless of how much could be believed, the parents wanted to help as much as possible in any way they could.

The meeting of fates was called to order. All of the children gathered around the small coffee table in the front room. They all sat cross-legged and put their heads together.

'So then, what is our best option?' Jade asked. 'We don't have a lot of options or a lot of time. We must think of something and something now'.

'Well, whatever it is, we need to tell them,' Becca reminded. 'Mr. and Mrs. Devon are scared to death about what I said concerning their son. They need to know we can be trusted to get him back for him. They want to know we'll be able to protect him'.

'Don't go promising things like that,' Alec advised.

'Yeah, but what do I tell them?' Becca asked.

'I don't want even to take a shot of answering that question,' Jade shuddered. She felt incredibly uncertain. No futures were easily predictable. At this point, if anything were going to happen, then it would for sure. No question.

Alec stood up and leaned on the fireplace. 'Time to end this madness plaguing us once and for all,' he declared with an authoritative voice.

'Well, no shit,' Hailey declared. 'But, how can we destroy a being possessed by The Devil. Can something like that even be done? I ask you. This isn't one of those creepy horror flicks'.

'Why do you keep asking these questions when you already know there isn't an answer?' Alec demanded, irritated in tone.

'Well, there must be something concrete that we can use as a weapon. Or a defence to say the least,' Jade thought. 'This thing can't be immortal if it has already died once before.'

'There's some truth in that statement,' Alec considered strongly.

Alec thought for a moment. Then, a thought occurred. 'I read a strange thing once before in the library,' he recalled.

'Go ahead,' Catherine offered. Alec, permitted, spoke of his idea to the crowd.

'From what I understand, a being possessed by The Devil can only be sent back to hell by either the one who placed it there or a being of blood.' For some, this sounded to be a rather strange idea. 'You have to be making that stuff up,' Becca denied. 'It killed Mr. Wilson, the man who locked her up in the room. It has been trying to take Wesley. And now she has. He is in the charms or so'.

'Nevertheless,' Alec maintained his theory. 'We have to take down this beast before there is more damage.'

The Van

Hailey had been sitting on the sofa contemplating the whole time. She had to think. As soon as Alec had finished speaking, the group got up from their seats, getting ready to go home. But, Hailey thought. There was something she needed to know. She went up to the boy and spoke.

'Say, Alec, might I ask you something?' She asked.

'You may ask me anything,' Alec said. 'What do you want to know? Go for it'.

Hilary cleared her throat to speak clearly.

'When you told us that scary story, you mentioned another incident as well. Something separate,' she stated. 'Something that had happened after the fire in the room.'

'Yes,' Alec considered. 'There were very several incidents that took place long after the death of The Devil Student in the fire,' he retorted vehemently. 'I am afraid you're going to have to be a little bit more specific on that detail.'

The young girl had to think extremely hard on this detail. 'You mentioned something about a van on the open road. Near the side of a canal. The driver caught sight of The Eyes and went over the side of an embankment, to the swamps below, to a watery grave'.

'That is true to that account,' Alec did not deny such a horrific event. 'Why are you bringing this up, lass?' He asked.

'Because there has to be a whole lot more to that story than that,' Hailey observed. She suspected something horrid. But, she was anxious and curious. 'Could you please tell us more, Al?'

'As you wish,' Alec agreed. He sat down in the living room on the old sofa. Hailey was still standing up. A few of the group was still around. They were comfortably huddled in the doorway. Alec thought about the story as he said it out loud.

'This would have been as least fifteen months after the incident within the Isolation Room. I cannot remember the exact date, but it must have been somewhere in May. This still strongly refers to the canal I spoke of. Mainly because that's where it happened. Men were carrying out refurbishing on the water edge. The work there needed an extra set of hands. Their department managed to hire a worker from the head office in London. Not much was known about him—only his appearance of overalls and a ginger beard. No name. Mainly kept himself to himself.

He was a hard-working man. Loved by those who knew him. He always looked to try any task thrown his way. He cared a significant amount about the road that he was working on. Yet, he was strongly aware that the lane down the waterfront was very unsafe for the crew. The tide of the canal was damaging the earth underneath the road, causing it to crumble. A foreman marked the spot where the ground was at its worst and weakest. Sadly, for the worker, the only transport he had for the trips was a van. That was way too heavy for the road.

It was surely not to end well for him'.

Hailey, Jade, and Caitlynn now emerged into the room all the way, given that they had been listening to the whole time. 'That's all noticeably clear for opening up. but, how did he end going into the canal then?' Caitlynn asked.

'Yeah,' Jade interjected. 'And how is all of this connected to The Eyes. Did he know anything about the story?'

'All in good time,' Alec protested. 'Please let me get to one thing at a time. Honestly, why do I always have to explain everything?' Despite this complaint, Alec continued with the story.

'This man was ordered to complete his work at the night shifts. Normally, he was known for finishing up on time. However, this was quite a bizarre night for him. It was completely pitch black. You probably couldn't make out a lighter under all the black darkness. Extremely late and pitch black. It was almost half-past eleven when he finally finished up, got into the van in question, and set off for home. The foreman who safeguarded the canal had to warn people about the unsafe road. He picked up the phone and tried to get his number. The van roared along the road like a lion chasing a gazelle. The worker was keen and determined to make up for the lost time and get home to his family before they were all in bed. Another workman tried to answer the telephone but couldn't hear the warning from the foreman. But, by the time he had got the message, it was already too late. The van was long gone in a quick, thick cloud of smoke. A shocking accident was waiting to happen'.

The team of teens was intrigued by what the boy was talking about. A nerving wave passed over the living room.

'It could only go from bad to worse from there,' Alec continued. 'It was a misty, cold moonlit night. When the driver reached the coast, his hopes for a fast run at it were driven down to the tarmac. Fog floated all over the screen. The van driver could not see a thing as he twisted and turned. When he could see down the road, it was too late.

And then, it happened'.

'Let me guess, dead,' Becca commented.

Ignoring the apparent end to the story, Alec continued the horrid tale.

'As the old van crossed over the canal, there appeared to be two amber objects merging from nowhere. The driver caught sight of these and lost control of his vehicle. The road surface crumbled from beneath him, and the van plunged over the side: Straight down into the murky raven below'.

'Jesus!' Hailey exclaimed.

'I guess the poor man died in that crash,' Jade assumed with a timid lisp in her mouth.

'Yes,' Alec agreed. 'His body was found by a passer-by. He was floating up. He was still covered in sticky gunge and his blood. The coroner declared him dead before the ambulance even took him away: Dead on impact. Eventually, he was laid to rest in a cemetery. The same one that now houses Gemma and Mr. Wilson. Many people who worked with him, employed him, and knew what was going on were called to court and practically sued for causing death by gross negligence'.

'And the van?' Becca asked. 'Where did the van go?'

'No one knows,' Alec commented. 'It was never found again. Some suggested that it rusted to shards of metal by the time people went looking for it. Or, it could be that the swamp was deeper than imagined. But, as I said, it was never found again. But many a worker will tell you that when the moon is pure and full up in the night sky, they have seen the van trying to get home across the dark canal.

But, it never reaches the other side'.

Every single adolescent around Alec shuddered as the story came to a haunting close. They held their voices, tongues, and breathes. It was surely a remarkable story. A strong light was shone on the legend of The Devil Student and what it was capable of.

All the same, Hailey thought there had to be something up. She finally broke the silence. 'There has to be a reason as to why the van was never found again.' She uttered this out loud. More mysteries were sure to ensue. What did The Eyes want with the canal? How were all of these atrocities possible?

Returned

The next morning, Alec Hanks made an exceedingly early start. He decided to make it count with a big long stroll across the beautiful countryside. It just so happened to be where the canal was. The tremendous edge of this countryside was the large hill. In his hand, Alec held a sword he got from the mantlepiece of his granddad. He explained to his older father, and he accepted the conditions of its use.

The sword belonged to him when he fought to the extreme in Vietnam. The sword wasn't too heavy. Alec had it strapped around his waist as he walked across the windy countryside. He could smell the horrid odour of the farm. Alec could feel that he was to be expected by a familiar foe: For an ominous black silhouette of a teenage boy, holding a long pole, was on the hilltop waiting for him, almost watching his footsteps come forward. Alec was sure that this person waiting for him was the blind child Phil Bridges.

The previous sleepless night, Alec had hatched a plan. He had to convince his present opponent that he was in the wrong. It was a strong thought to persuade Phil to come into a better and brighter light. It would be this firm revival that would lend his team a greater upper hand, bringing Phil to his senses and be a catalyst in bringing down The Devil Student and her reign of terror before it even began and spread over.

It was to be a lethal gamble, indeed.

Phil was indeed waiting for him. He looked over the slope of the hill to see Alec come closer and closer. Alec stopped when he was directly facing his glasses. He raised the sword. It was within centimetres of his neck.

'Is this what it has come down to?' Phil asked. 'Fighting like rabid animals. You were expecting to win a fight with me'.

'It's a good measure,' Alec said. 'There is an obvious advantage.'

'What advantage do you have over me?' Phil said arrogantly. He moved his rival's weapon away from him as he circled him. 'What does an over-confident boy like you have to bring to a party of weak teenagers?'

'Playground insults are not going to be enough this time,' Alec defied. 'It doesn't have to be this way. You can let go of this hatred. There is no shame in doing the right thing'.

'What right things have this neighbourhood done?' Phil asked.

'This was all you and that witch thing,' Alec coughed. 'You and The Eyes have caused nothing but trouble. So much pain has come as a consequence. The Eyes have killed so many people out of fear, terror, and prejudice against its own sick life'.

'Several more shall follow them in this conquest overall matter,' Phil promised. 'More and more until the entire world is ours. You will either join us in respect and obedience. Or you will be claimed by Hell and die screaming at the feet of The Devil himself'.

Alec was not amused at Phil's ignorant behaviour towards such a serious atrocity on the rise. 'You can go straight to hell,' he cried out. With his grandfather's sword in hand, he lashed out at Phil. As the blade came crashing down, the visually impaired boy morphed his hands slowly together. This was able to create a sword of his own: One that was highly decorated and looked incredibly sharp. Quick as a whip, Phil dived out of the way and blocked the blow with his weapon.

'Very well, go on then,' he snarled crossly. 'Do what you must, boy. Let's have at it with you'.

Both of the boys raced at each other and lashed out with their swords with murderous intent. They made their steps sideways as to counter each other's attacks. They swung back and forth and leaned in and out to dodge and attack each other with their weapons. Alec ducked and dived to avoid the lethal blade. He felt the burn of fires across his back. He thrust the sword forward in many different ways and directions. He tried to land as many cuts on Phil as possible. His blind opponent was not duly impressed at his idleness, and how he handled the weapon as if it was a classy toy. They launched themselves at each other. The impact of this sent them rolling down the hill.

Phil got up first and shook himself of dust and debris. He felt very dizzy at what he had just done. He looked down on his foe with a feeling of disgust in his eye. He did not tolerate the boy's sloppiness. 'Pathetic!' He wrote off as he towered over the guy. 'You look far weaker than you pretend yourself to be.' He gloated rudely as he kicked him in the chest. 'You would be inadequate for The Devil.'

Alec jumped to his feet. Still feeling a throbbing under his shirt, he swung the blade around above the boy's head as he dodged. They both used one hand each to land attacks on each other. They spun back to back on each other and pushed each other away. Alec blocked fierce blows and shoved the blind assailant away from him with a sharp punch. They joined their swords together with both hands and spun around each other. Phil leaned in and elbowed the boy across the field.

They then held their weapons above their heads and chanced each other dead in the eyes. Phil launched Alec backward, spinning him. He brought down the blade; Alec swerved to the side. They fought at each other in great power. The intense duel took both of them down the embankment beside the lake. Alec inched Phil closer to falling and pressed hard on his sword to force him. Phil held for dear life, and he reached a free hand down and sprayed his attacker with cold water. Alec's reaction was fierce, forcing him to move back.

Both fighters inched away from the lake and looked at each other face to face.

'I do not want to fight you like this, dude,' Alec pleaded for his opponent's common sense. 'Can't you see a better way to live than this? Do you not have any idea what Molly will do to our world?'

Phil responded with the strongest belief he knew. 'Death, my friend, is the only freedom I can ever accept. You have no idea what it feels like in my world'. Phil swung the sword on him. They went up and down each other until Alec elbowed him back. Bleeding from his lips, Phil coughed up. 'As a boy, I knew nothing. I had no closure. I will have that when I knock you to the dirt'

Alec scowled at such an idea. Phil rushed forward to slice at his arm. Alec caught his waist and tipped him over onto his back. He hit the ground with a massive thud. Alec brought his sword down on him for a killing strike. Phil blocked it. He tried to stab the boy standing, but Alec moved back. Alec launched an onslaught of strikes at his foe. Both boys fought for all that they were capable of. The blind child seemed to be faster than what Hanks imagined. He swung his weapon and made it come alight. It struck Alec straight in his right shoulder blade. The victim of such a strike screamed as a large red rash became visible all of his upper arms and spread for his chest.

'When will you learn?' Phil asked as he taunted close to his ears. 'When will you learn your lessons?' He snapped. 'If the truth is to be told, there is no chance or point in saving anyone. Yet, you never give up. That is an issue that greatly bothers me'.

He charged up. Quick as a whip, Alec jumped up and pulled up a dagger from the back of his jeans. He waved both the sword and the dagger back and forth in different turns. Phil was rather nervous at what his opponent was bringing out at random moments of a lethal duel. Alec shook the dagger, and it became a large sword shaped weapon. He waved them both around at fast paces. Phil tried to catch the speeds and spun around his foe with great conviction. There was so much to keep track of as he tried to avoid being hit by both blades. Alec waved them up and down, one after the other, and faced him dead straight in the eyes as he forced him towards the lake again.

Phil tried to gain more strength as he went. He tried to keep in pattern with both swords. Alec was beginning to lose his breathe fast. His opponent was too fast and more advanced in his skills. Phil spun his dagger sword to the left and kicked it out of the way.

'Are you ready to give it in, boy?' Phil growled gruffly to him. Alec denied such a thought as he grabbed for his other weapon. He combined them both into one sword. He waved them around the other guy's device. He displayed a massive amount of power in his speed as a swordsman as he made a massive slice across his opponent's chest. Phil reacted loudly as the blade touched him.

Phil tried to charge straight up to his foe. Alec moved himself to be in front of the murky lake. Just as Phil's blade came in close, Alec dodged from his way, causing the blind felon to land himself in the watery gunge.

'Now, will you listen to me, you crazed bastard?' Alec asked down below.

Phil was now soaking wet. He tried to stand up in the lake among the gooey waters. He tried to shake his sword and make it powerful. However, it was now a mouldy stick pulled from the branch of a tree. No matter how hard he shook it, no matter what he tried to do, the branch would not do anything strong at all.

'You have to listen to me now,' Alec pleaded with him passionately. He looked into his cloudy eyes to see a good man. 'We have a lot in common, dude. You and I come from the same horrid neighbourhood. We both know about the story of The Eyes. We know how to defeat them, save our boy Wesley Devon and everyone here.

Our lives depend on it. Do you not see that, you crazy horse?'.

Phil did not appreciate this tone. He decided to make himself utterly blank in his facial expression. Not a motion of feeling was portrayed. Alec snapped his fingers in front of his face.

'Come on, listen to me, Phillip.' Alec pleaded as if he was an eight-year-old child wanting his dad to buy a toy. 'Do you not want to live to at least feel tomorrow? Are you that detached from the life you go to the darkness? We need you to help us set things right again'.

Alec held out his hand. The defeated took it as he crawled out of the water and shook himself dry. He maintained his rant of grief.

'You have no idea what it is like to live in a world the way I do. You know that I have been blind all my life. I have always been made to feel low and unaccepted'.

'Yes, I know,' Alec agreed. 'I stood up for you when you were attacked the night before. You deserve better than what you have been given. But I want you with us. I can see how you've always wanted to do good. But, being with the horrid evil like The Eyes is not going to help you. I think you know that deep inside yourself.

I wish I knew how all of that felt for you. Maybe, if you came with me, we could put an end to all of this whole hell. Then, I think you would have the closure and acceptance you have longed for. Does that sound fair?'

Phil sounded like the logic was true. He took his hand, and the two of them walked away back to their basis.

The Last Dark Night of the Life

Shortly after that, having dusted each other off with the gungy lake water and dust from the grass, both of the boys, made their ways slowly back to the house of Devon. When the doorbell rang out across the porch, Hailey was the one to open the door on them. When she did so, she was livid to see such a treacherous slime on the arm of a dear friend. She was very keen to help smooth and cool the burn marks on Alec and patch up all the cuts of everyone.

'What is he doing here?' Hailey asked. 'Did you suddenly go blind? No offence, Phil'.

'None taken,' Phil denied. 'I didn't want it to be like this. I didn't want any of this to happen'. He apologised deeply. 'It is for pity's sake that I decided to give into Alec's skills with his sword. I have decided that I am going to join with you. In the hope that all of this hell can be suppressed for good this time. All of us are not so different after all'.

'Why should we trust anything you say from here on?' Becca asked. 'You have gone insane. You have lived in a world of evil with Molly'.

'You think I am proud of this,' Phil said. 'I want no more of this. I want peace, not destruction. And I have more information you. You need to hear me out, please.'

The school children listened to the blind child's words with great care. There seemed to be a great texture of urgency. There was something they had not been told yet at all.

'Our world is on fire,' Phil described. 'I cannot see the flames, yet I know they are there. I can just smell the horrid smoke and tell how the world is decaying beneath our feet. Molly Devon's wrath will spread its way through every-where until there is no good to see or be left in this world'.

'What is the problem there?' Jade protested. 'She's only a ghostly spirit. She's been dead for years'.

'As far as this part of the world knows, death has no value anymore,' Phil snorted. 'She's just as volatile dead as she ever was alive. We've all seen how powerful she can be'.

'Nevertheless, a spirit is hard to kill,' Caitlynn commented on an indisputable fact. 'It is not so simple just to wipe her out. We're not ghostbusters, and Alec is not as stupid and impossible as Bill Murray'.

'Boatload of humour you are,' Alec said sarcastically.

'There's no question. It's us or the world. It has to be us together that take her down. I'm sorry, we are devoid of choice'.

Becca could not be any more stressed out if she tried. She had finally had enough of the same monotonous comments over this cursed indenture. It almost felt like they couldn't talk about anything else. She stood up on the footstool and made enough noise to silence them all. They all turned their heads towards her as she spoke.

'Can't you guys SHUT THE HELL UP!' She snapped crossly.

'What's your problem now?' Jade asked.

'Just listen to yourselves,' Becca said. 'All of you are just ready to give in to this thing. Just ready to give up and go into that thing and die. What is the point with that stuff?'

'What point are you trying to make here?' Her sister asked in great awe.

'The point is that it doesn't have to be like this. We don't just have to go in without a plan. These things can be changed by us, yes. But, there is a chance for us to get back to light and see the next day'.

'Your compassion is as false as your nails,' Caitlynn scoffed.

Phil twitched his head suddenly. A thought began to materialise inside his brain. The group noticed this a lot. 'Are you alright, Phil?' Hailey asked. 'Do you need something?'

'No, I'm fine,' Phil said. 'I have heard of one possible way to vanquish The Devil Student. Permanently this time,' he uttered.

'What you do mean, Bridges?' Jade asked. She felt confident he was entirely on their side.

The blind boy spoke as clearly and as calmly as he could.

'Someone would have to charge at the horrible thing with a metal object of some description. A bit like a sword, possibly. I'd say one slice of such would be enough. The Devil Student would be gone in a flash'.

Everyone in the room was very intrigued in what was being suggested here. Their eyes were certainly lit up in admiration. It like there was a saviour on the otherwise bleak horizon.

'Then, if that's fair, that's what you have to do,' Hailey firmly declared.

But, just when people were smiling and looking up for once, Phil raised his hand, as if to speak again.

'However, like everything you have gone over so far, there is a deadly price involved,' he said.

'Oh, come on, what now?' Alec sighed.

Phil sighed very deeply as he spoke the cost of potential success.

'Any such person who takes the valiant charge towards The Devil Student will die in the Never world of Hell with Molly herself. Whoever it is will die too.

I'm sorry it sounds like that. Like every other option, your mind, it all ends badly. It's a suicide mission for you'.

Hailey's volume in her words returned to the helm of the room. She felt very indignant and impatient.

'I honestly do not care anymore. I do not care for suicide. We might as well be all dead if we're not gonna stand up to The Devil Student,' she said powerfully. 'If there is any chance to bring back poor Wesley, we have to do it. It is our duty as his friends. He deserves better than to be trapped as a servant to his ghost sister'. She gulped and swallowed nervously as she spoke out loud, 'A life can be made right.'

Hailey insisted on the strong plea with great venom in her stomach. She had never spoken with so much passion before. It almost hurt her to talk the way she had done. Her friends and family were left nervous. The familiar touch of her younger sister was felt on her shoulder blade.

'You like him as much as I do?' She asked.

'Yes,' came the simple reply. 'I would give my ass to get him back to the light.'

'So would I,' Alec agreed. 'Wesley and I grew up together. I would risk myself to save him. Tonight, we'll strike at the school. This will be awesome. It will be extremely tough. But, the fate of everything good in beautiful depends on it'.

The Last Strike

This is where the group of heroic teens united against the forces of evil. Dark thick clouds grew overhead as the night was on its way. Alec, Hailey, and the whole entourage of the team made their hellish strides towards the towering school building. The solitary lights for them to see within the closed school institution was the eerie white glow from the locker corridor and the fearsome yellow spread of light from the roof of the second floor of the giant stairwell. Sneaking past the security cameras above, the team broke into the building through the door opposite the hall of lockers.

Alec used a lock pick to prize open all the locked doors generally opened by a key card by a member of staff. They were now in the creepy stair chasm. They began to climb the steps one by one. With every step they took, a strange vibration could be heard. They were old structures; It should be worth mentioning. The stair safety had not been checked in a long while.

It was now on the first level: The history floor. The team was now feeling very wobbly weakened in their knees. The fact they were even there in the first place was enough to question their sanities as a group.

'I hate this, you guys.' Becca shuddered as if she was standing in the arctic with no warm clothes on. 'You guys feel the same?'

'Yeah, I feel it.' Her sister whispered as she took hold of her hand. 'The feeling is mutual. It wanted us just as much as it wanted Wes. We have to do it now. It has to be now'.

Alec came forward towards the edge of the stairs. It looked very dark as he gazed around the perimeter.

'Devon!' He called out to summon up the enemy. 'The un-measurable hell that you have caused over us all ends as now. You have torn us apart and turned us against each other for days on end. No more of that, now. Come out now and show yourselves'.

As Alec said this haunting command, the fog outside the school building began to roll in slowly. It slowly began to grow still. It was at this point where it all occurred.

The fire door below the stairwell opened up with a squeak in the end. The wind seeped through with a sinister whirl. It grew very cold all around the teens. Jade pointed long and far as the outline of a little girl in the middle of the stairs. It looked orange and red as the face of evil emerged. Her figure looked as it did when The Eyes transformed earlier and took hold of Wesley. she stepped forward and spoke in an icy voice.

'Here I am, foolish mortals,' she addressed. Her dangerous energy emerged slowly and enveloped the school. The spar-kle of it could be seen for miles around the area. 'How dare you summon me on such poorness!' She snapped angrily as she took full shape as a human being. 'All of you are fools to take me on like this. And fools are what you will perish as'.

Alec tried to stay as confident as possible. He spoke in a strange behaviour to her and everyone behind him.

'So, you won't stay in the grave, will you now?' Alec ob-served.

'I shall never die at all,' The Devil Student declared. 'The Devil within me will never be extinguished. I am the eternal force of all that is evil in this world. You will become a chan-nel of it as such'.

Molly looked over across the stairway towards Phil. She growled in disgust at his betrayal.

'I expected a lot better from you,' she snarled. 'You were my best chance of destroying this world. I could've given you power beyond your capability. I could've granted you respect, joy for the rest of your life. I could've even given you the chance to see your mum for the first time. Take a look at me. This life you helped well to destroy'.

'Don't listen to her, it's all lies,' Caitlynn urged. 'She's messing with your head. Just like with everyone already'.

Phil was having none of this as he nodded to Caitlynn and spun back to the supernatural beast. 'I should like to take a moment to say that I am not going to listen of any more of this tomfoolery at the idea that we were the reason behind your death in that fire…'

'None of us were even at high school then,' Hailey interrupted.

'…Yeah,' Phil Bridges continued. 'It was all your fault for how obscene you acted. I was wrong about grand you are. You're a savage sociopath, bitch!'

Molly smirked cruelly. 'It satisfied me that I should make my way to the next realm of existence. That I have my full powers overall'.

Alec was beginning to find this insufferable.

'The only real thing that would ever satisfy you was being on top of everything like a queen,' Alec snorted. 'You had every chance to get your act together, bub. But, you never accepted any of it. You always wanted to be the centre of attention. You refused to mend your ways and paid the price. Now, look where you are.

I see now strongly how you are not just an evil ghost: You are a savage fucking beast. There is nothing in your being but pure hatred'.

'Hatred indeed,' Molly responded. 'Hatred that has kept me going. Keeping my soul intact all this time'.

'Soul? SOUL!' Hailey screamed out. 'What soul? There is no soul in you at all. That can end here right now'.

Molly scoffed some more. 'Very well. If it is your choice to not give into my will, I guess I shall have to destroy you all where you stand'.

Molly raised her arms and conjured her powers.

Alec felt very pompous and taunted her, foolishly. 'What are you going to do?' He dared. 'Freeze us to the floor. Bring it on, you son of a bitch'.

Phil felt quite bored with all the conversation taking place. 'Alright, I've had enough of this.'

Out of his blind faith, Phillip Bridges drew his sword up high. He stepped forward unaided and took a fearless run up and brought the sword down in a slashing motion, trying to slice The Devil Student in half. But, before the killing blow could be executed. Molly morphed out of the way in a dis-embodied motion, laughing evilly as she did it.

'Come you now, you little beast,' Phil raged as he lashed out some more. There was not an ounce of effort into it as the rest of the team tried to help him out. The effect was to no avail. Molly felt very sure of herself as she revelled in her advantage. She kept dodging until Phil was worn out. At such point, she just pushed him to the floor.

'You have no capability of destroying me.' She rejoiced. 'You are weak. Is this all you have to offer? If this is the case, it is a benefit that you are both blind and have opted to fight against me'.

Then, it was the turn of Hailey Southerland.

She tried to strike her as well with a sword that was just as sharp, and at speed similar to Phil's. She took a great leap off the side of the wall as if to come crashing down on the villain as well. Alas, the effort in this leap of faith was of no avail. Molly caught hold of her legs as she began to make land. She sent the violent attacker spinning until she found herself being thrown, hitting the wall she took off from. There was a loud thump as her head came into contact with the thick wall. She slumped quickly to the floor, motionless but breathing softly.

Her sister panicked as she rushed to her side to check her.

Alec was not amused at what he was witnessing. 'There was no need for you to do that!' He began to lose his rag with her. Molly morphed her way towards him.

'I think you will find, sonny, that there was every need for me to do that,' she gloated in an oily tone.

'And, to your answer the question you had earlier.'

Alec tried to back away: Closer to the door of the History department. Suddenly, he felt himself stick. His shoes were stuck to the floor he stood at. He could tell something horrid was about to happen.

'W…w…w…what are you doing?' He panicked up in fear as he felt the rest of his body slip. He was beginning to sink into the floor. He looked as if he was completely paralysed. Molly towered over him. She held out her hand over him as if to cast a spell on him.

'You are forever mine now,' she taunted cruelly. 'This is where and how you will pay the price for your insolent be-haviour.'

Alec shook himself as he tried to move away. 'You can go straight to Hell for this.'

Molly responded to him. 'I am already there. You will join me there now. And you will stay with me there for the rest of your miserable life'.

Alec shut his eyes as she reached in close with a ball of energy.

Just then, there was a loud crunch above them. A possessed Wesley Devon stormed through the doors on the next high floor. He dived down, and he landed beside the demonic sister of his. His evil, hell-bound energy soared from his body. He looked like a villain version of Hellboy. He morphed up a sword out of his hand. Like the one Phil used against Hanks, it was covered in flames of boiling fire.

'As if we couldn't guess,' Becca said. 'Couldn't you bring him out earlier?'

'It's no fun if you know it's coming,' Phil said. He was still trying to catch his breathe.

'This is why I was always one step ahead of you the whole time.' Molly explained how Wesley had indirectly played a part in the destruction. 'I had my brother at school. He never even knew his parents had had children before himself. He never knew my legends at first hand. I gave him little hints to enter my telling: The heat across the landscape; The looming over in the exam hall; The incidents in the bathroom and the corridor. All the was needed to ice the cake was him being told the story by his own best friend.

It seemed to me that the more Wesley learned about myself, the easier it became to reach out to him and those he loves. It was all too easy for him to fall under my powers: Just by casually catching him off guard. And not, he is mine to control and manipulate. He can now do my will and rule with me. Having the power, he always wanted'.

Alec tried to crane his head up. 'DON'T YOU SEE, WES!' Alec screamed and coughed up out as he tried to resist the friction. 'You are nothing but a massive stupid pawn in her schemes. She is just using you to poor ends. And when she takes the world over in evil, she will destroy you in one go'.

'You are just jealous of him, son,' Molly snarled and gave the most haunting evil laugh heard. She sounded like a costumed witch. 'You could have stood by my side like your friend has, you stupid bonehead. But, with your poor attitude, I can now see a glorious victory ahead'.

Molly held out her hand straight and morphed a ball of lightning. Just as Alec began to get up back onto his feet, she fired the fireball fast at Alec's feet. It blew the shocked boy off his feet. He looked up while covered in plaster.

'You have no strength at all. You may as well give in to the fates and die a man. No one will know'.

Alec yelled his ground as he held up his sword as high as he could reach. He said, 'Why don't you come over here and kiss my ass!'

Molly's Evil Eyes boiled up with an angry red.

'WHY, YOU HORRID LITTLE INGRATE!'

The following fight was a three-way struggle between Alec Hanks, The Devil Student, and her possessed brother Wesley. The three of them began to fight each other at great speed and tenacity. Becca, Caitlynn and Jade tried to revive Hailey as the three attackers tried to defend and fight each other to the deaths. Phil was just coming to her senses and get his strength back. He lunged forward with a cheer. Molly forced him back with a bolt of devil energy straight into his face. This sent him off course. He lost his balance and fell from view. Becca raced to see if he was hurt at all.

The hands of the fighters were a blur. The ways they swirled their swords around were unpredictable and extremely violent. They twirled back and forth against each other, making strong contact with their blades. Alec spun around both of the attackers. He tried to force them away from each other as he picked them off. They struck back and forth until Wesley knocked Alec backward. Molly began to gang upon him. She tried to strike him down with a slice above his head. Obviously, she missed it.

Alec picked up another sword and tried to even the scores of the fighting. He swung them around both of the Devon siblings.

'Please listen to me,' he pleaded to Wesley as he dodged the blade of fire. He swung back and forth between the tiny space. He tried to separate both of the foes, and he knocked them down for them to get up again. They both swung over his head, and he ducked low. They stood off against him.

Molly handed her brother her sword. Wesley charged at his best friend and tried to lash out in the ways of his friend. Hailey was just getting back her strength. She rushed to Wesley's arm and kissed him on the cheek. Wesley felt it and knocked the girl away again. Alec tried to keep up the rest of the fight. But, it was way too much. There came a large cut across his back as he spun on the spot. This ended his chances to do more damage. Down he fell to the floor, front first.

Molly felt enormously proud of herself for what had just happened. 'Finish the job, my brother,' she taunted.

But, she wasn't counting on something that was twirling inside Wesley's head. His mind began to clear slowly. The mental powers of his sister quickly began to fade away. His eyes changed colour to their natural state. Wesley Devon had been brought back to normality. He then turned on his sister with all his might and fought back against his control.

'What have you done?' She raged crossly at yet another betrayal. 'You cannot even rely on your own family. You just took down your best friend. You couldn't even give me a minute to enjoy that?' She snarled.

'No,' Wesley bluntly said. 'What is there for anyone to enjoy now? This was not a place I love anymore. All because of your evil. You have never been, and you never will be, my sister. And now, I'm going to take my shot on you'.

'Just one slice on my with that thing, and I am gone forever. Yet you will be too,' Molly tested.

Wesley saw his chance. With his word raised high, and his newfound power of his own in him, he lunged forward.

'Don't do it,' Hailey said as she rose to her feet once more. 'It'll kill you.'

'I don't care,' Wesley said. Hailey shielded her eyes tight. Wesley ran in fast. With one last cheer, he yelled 'GO BACK TO HELL, YOU SON OF A BITCH!' he swung his iron sword. Her neck was sliced open, the pool of evil blood poured out and ran down fast. Wesley sliced with the sword again, and there was a terrible flash of white light.

When the smoke from the flash had drifted away, the Devil Student was nowhere to be seen. Everyone got back to their feet and cheered in glee. The power of the rigid iron sword had disrupted the energy of The Devil Student, forcing her to go back to hell. Along with everything else she has brought with her and had caused.

In a nearby canal, pieces of rusted iron floated to the top. They showed the remains of a vehicle crashed there long ago.

Then, all of a sudden, Wesley Devon began to feel incredibly weakened from the forehead down to the edge of his knees. He slowly collapsed in a heap on the floor. His head was positioned dangerously over the edge of the top stair. Hailey, Caitlynn, Jade, Becca, and Phil all rushed and knelt at his side. Alec helped prop his head up on one of his old pillows he'd taken for the journey.

'Hi there,' he coughed up as he breathed his last slowly.

'It's too late,' Phil said. 'The damage has already been done' as he watched steam leave his body as it does from a kettle.

'By killing The Devil Student in the way he did,' Jade had begun to theorise again. 'He pretty much took all the life out of himself.'

'It's fine, buddy, you did it well, mate,' Alec smiled.

'There was no other way I could end this,' Devon coughed in whatever breathes he had left. 'But, at least I did one last good thing in my life. And I got to be with my friends and meet my sister. One last time'.

The friends watched and listened deeply with tears to Wesley's last words. He slumped back onto the floor for his final sleep.

Dead.

Concluding Statements

What a shocking relief it all was. Everyone was happy that The Devil Student's reign of terror had ended. An ambulance arrived at the school building as the sky began to clear up. The crystal blue sky emerged with a sun shining with warm and content temperatures. Phil was taken to the hospital on account of his special ordeal. The team followed closely. Wesley's lifeless body was taken away as well to the same place for examination. The teens were next seen together in the hospital waiting room. Phil laid on a single bed alone. The manipulation of The Devil Student's energy had something very lethal to his eyes.

At long last, a doctor came out into the hallway. He was carrying a clipboard and had major news to tell. Several of the friends stood up from the bench and had their teeth gritted, expecting the worst.

'How is he doing in there?' Alec asked with anxiety clutching his throat.

The doctor described the irregular condition he was faced into.

'He'll be alright. Just be glad he is alive. He made it through sure enough. If you would like to see for yourself, you are welcome to go in and take a look'.

At this point, all of them were stood up. The teens went into the hospital ward. Once they found the section that he was in, all of them were huddled around his bed. He was lying still as ice. He had a clean white cloth over his forehead: His eyes were covered.

Phil could feel his friends come close to him. They all knelt at his bedside. The traumatised boy was helped to sit up by one of the surgeons, for he was in a great dizzy state of mind.

He put his hands up across his forehead to feel the silk cloth across his eyes. He ran his hands around it towards the back, finding a double knot at the back. With a small fiddle, he untied the knot and removed the cloth. It fell from reach at the side of the bed. He felt water coming from his eyes, and he wiped it off. He blinked a couple of times. From how he looked, it looked like a classic, fuzzy television screen.

'I have to be dreaming somehow,' he coughed in a confused tone. 'Is this all real? Where am I?' He turned towards the face of a young girl who was leaning over his bed rail. 'Hailey? Hailey Southerland? Is it truly you? Have you always had your hair like that?' He asked.

Hailey was alarmed at how he was acting out. The teenage guests did not know what they could believe here. How was this transformation possible? For such a lowly boy, who had been blinded since the day he was born, to be able to see for the very first time. This was a truly extraordinary achievement to behold.

'How can he suddenly now see?' Caitlynn asked.

'It's hard to think that,' Jade thought studiously. 'It is common for blind people to gain their sight back.'

'Give or take treatment,' Phil coughed. 'Plus trauma recovery.'

'I suppose you could say he has his sight due to residual powers for The Eyes,' Jade assumed. 'This is no measure of human abilities.'

'I'd say that you are half right on that one.' Alec credited the forward-thinking. 'If you think about it, both Phil and The Eyes both have what the other one needs: A body and sight.'

'Whatever the case, he now sees,' Hailey smiled. 'That's a good enough point for a great life.'

'Yet, he looks like he's had a stroke,' Becca thought. 'You can lose your sight if you suffer from a stroke.'

'Don't you worry about that, Hailey.' The Doctor advised. 'He'll be fine. Just give him as much care as he needs. Now, if you could excuse me, I need to find the discharge forms'.

And he left.

As soon as he had left the area, the teens continued with the rest of their questions and socialising as much as possible.

'So, how do you feel now?' Hailey asked.

Phil still felt as flustered as his friends were. They had no idea as to what they had all gone through. 'To be honest, Hailey, I don't know yet. Sixteen years ago, my mother was crying her eyes out when she heard the diagnosis that I was born blind. Now I'll be able to see her for the first time. I wish there were some explanations for all of this.

Maybe there are no explanations for stuff like this'.

Alec's face felt entirely blank in what he was seeing and thinking of. But then, ever so slightly, a small idea formed in his mind.

'You still have the powers of The Eyes. I don't suppose you could use your powers just to bring back Wesley Devon'. He joked casually as he knew himself. It sounded ridiculous. 'He is only over by the window in the next room. I don't suppose it is possible to give him life again'.

'Are you sure you know what you're saying?' Becca asked.

'I think so,' Alec was nervous in his ideas. He didn't know.

Phil thought hard. 'I think it could be possible. Could some of you help me up?'

Caitlynn and Jade helped the young lad up. Becca offered him his cane. He rejected it. Looked at his arms for the first time; he could see they were glowing yellow. The teens helped him down the next room. They found the poor boy lying lifeless on the bed at the end of the room. Phil placed a hand on his forehead. He put the other hand on his stomach. The last of the enchanted energy flowed into the dead body. Everyone stood back and waited for any results. It was worth watching as his body twitched, as if with life returning to young Wesley.

'Well, something's happening,' Becca observed.

She was not wrong. Wesley's eyes slowly began to open up. As if he was getting up for bed in the morning. He gasped for breath as he slowly sat up. It was as if he had been held down at the deep end of a swimming pool.

'I sure as heck cannot believe this.' He gasped in disbelief. He felt his flesh all over his body. It was as dry as a clean tea towel, And as ice-cold as a tub of ice cream in a freezer.

The revived boy looked around the hospital room. And there were his friends standing at his side. He opened his mouth, and he said, 'Did I just go skinny dipping in the arctic?'

'Yep, he's back alright,' Alec smiled casually.

Hailey was over the moon and incredibly happy at what had just occurred. She rushed forward and wrapped her arms around the boy in a massive hug of pure happiness. Wesley felt delighted at this. He felt thrilled that he was even alive in the first place.

'Good to have you back, bruv.' Alec commented with a grin and casual fist bump.

'I love that, dude,' Devon said as he tried to stand up once more. It felt natural as it would be. 'Where have I been? The last thing I knew, I was staring at an outline of my sister. Wait, I had a sister?'

'Yes, you did have a sister,' Alec confirmed. 'It's an awfully long story. We are all only glad that you have come back to us safe and sound'.

Becca sneaked out of the room for a short moment.

Devon thought hard for a moment. Then, he remembered something from the days before. 'The Eyes! The Eyes! It's not a person or a ghost. It's a powerful entity. It feeds on what people fear, think, and what they have learned about it. Hence the reason Mr Wilson was killed. He knew everything about them. he is the one who put them away for good. I guess Gemma was just a horrid silly accident. Unless, of course, she knew something as well'.

'No one knows,' Hailey stated. 'I guess we never will.'

'Maybe that is for the best at these times of reflection,' Becca said as she arrived. She had urgent news. 'Your parents know what has happened. They will be very overwhelmed to see what's happened'.

She was not wrong at all.

And it was at this point that the young Wesley Devon was released from his hospital room along with Phil Bridges. They were now allowed to return to their respective families. Those families in question were waiting for them back in the hospital halls. Devon knew his parents were there even before he ran up to them to hug them. He could strongly tell form the shameful expressions on their faces that they had a lot of explanations to be told.

Naturally, everyone hugged each other with glee.

'Neither of us could bear the thought of you being killed,' his dad Peter observed. 'But, when the new headmaster, Mr. Goodman, told me that you might still be alive, we had to see for ourselves. It is clear our prayers have been answered'.

Their son gave a sweet smile. 'I never knew I had a sister. I can't possibly believe the cruel way she acted out. How come you never told me about her?'

'There's not much reason why we didn't tell you. It did bring up a lot of horrid memories. Those memories could scar anyone. Even an innocent boy like you'. His mum, Natalie, said. 'But, don't you worry, son. It's ok. The good that was still in her, that once was, now thrives in the good boy you were always born to be'.

'And what's more,' Peter Devon added. 'You'll make an even greater older brother when your mother gives birth to our beautiful baby come this August'.

Wesley was amazed at this news.

Hailey, on the other hand, had gone very silent. Her younger sister had noticed this for a good while.

'Hailey, is everything ok with you?' She asked silently.

Hailey sniffed. 'This is a lot of crazy for me now. Now that Wesley is back from the dead. And Phil has his sight again. Now I have no idea who I go to the prom with. I had already settled from Alec for some time. Alec, Phil, and Wesley have all shown themselves to be strong, brave, and brilliant gents. Do I seriously have to pick one?'

'Not necessarily,' Phil had been listening to this predicament for the last while. 'I didn't tell this. I'm going to the dance with Caitlynn Missin. But, you could ask both Alec Hanks and Wesley Devon.

I'm sure they would be more than happy to take you'.

'He's very right to that end.' Alec and Wesley said in unison. 'We would both be more than happy indeed.'

Hailey beamed, and all three of them hugged in significant agreement.

Prom

Sure enough, after much needed time to relax, the big day came around very quickly indeed. The lights shining across the room, the party food spread across the tables, the loud pop music blaring out of the speakers, all the pretty prom dresses with none of them matching: It looked like such a brilliant way to end off the long five years of secondary school. It was a lot of luck. The school had been re-opened in time.

Wesley Devon was keen to make a great entrance on this grand occasion. To himself for how positively he had improved, he hit the school grounds in a posh limousine. Devon was pleased he was alive again and was ready to live life to its fullest once again. The crowd proceeded to erupt in massive applause when he emerged from the limo. Devon did a large lap of the car to open all the doors on the outside, as to allow his guests to emerge their own glory as well. Alec, Hailey and Jade exited and were met with great responses. Becca was waiting around the cargo rails to see her sister in her lilac coloured dress. This dress reflected strongly against the shine of the limo and the blue and white suits of the respective date, Alec and Wesley.

Following the arrival of these 4, a 1970 Ford Mustang Boss 429 emerged. Phil and Caitlynn walked out of the car. Phil was wearing a burgundy coloured suit with a black bow tie, while Caitlynn was wearing a dress, coloured pink: An excellent match for this.

The great dance went down very well. It was strongly elegant and a great time for everyone. There were lots of couples, trios, and other prom groups scattered around the dance hall together. It was strongly beautiful, touching, and cosy. Phil required Caitlynn Missin to lead him across the dancefloor, and anywhere else for that matter. His sight, while good enough to read a book and watch a film and TV, was still incredibly weak. The bright lights were awkward and hard to deflect the gaze.

But, honestly, Phil didn't care much about how bright it was. He was glad he could finally see people, the sun in the sky, and God's beautiful creatures for the very first time in a long age.

Caitlynn was pleased to see how far Phil had come in respect to how alone he had been forced to be since birth. But now, he had the respect and closure he had longed for in the longest time ever.

Wesley stood outside on the school balcony. He took a deep breath of fresh night-time air. The night out was just absolutely beautiful. The stars lit up the night sky in a, fantastic vision. He smiled as if he had never done before. He was subsequently joined by his best mate, Alec Hanks. He was carrying a glass of lemonade in his hand.

'So, when was the last time a guy like you stopped to appreciate the night sky like this, old boy?' He asked this in a posh manner as he could fake. He was looking too; At the scenes of beautiful lit houses as far as he could visualise.

'I can't say if I remember or not,' Wesley replied.

Alec decided to change the subject. 'Hailey's in there. Waiting for you. Why don't you go and give her a dance? You have always wanted to'.

Wesley reacted with a scratch on the back of his neck. 'I should like to state for the record, I do not fancy Hailey. I never did. Yes, she kissed me. So what? Girls are not important to me yet. But, as I always say, never say never'. Wesley decided to deflect the awkward question onto him.

'What about you, Alec? Do you have anyone in mind?'

Alec scoffed in as much embarrassment as the boy opposite.

'I'm openly asexual anyway, mate. You should know that,' Alec accepted and declared. 'It doesn't matter to me.' He calmed his tone down. 'I missed you every hour you weren't with us.'

'I missed you too,' Wesley said. 'I couldn't imagine you being hurt. And I'm sorry I did'.

'No need for you to worry about that,' Alec smiled.

Just then, Mr. Goodman, newly appointed headmaster, emerged to see the boys.

'Aren't you going to get in there while the night is young?' He encouraged very slyly. Both boys sniggered as they escorted each other into the room. The prom awards were going to be announced. Phil won the best suit while Hailey earned the best dress. Wesley won prom king, but he rejected the award, giving it to his best friend. This came at an ironic move when Alec was giving the award of Prom Prince. It was quite a strange thing, indeed.

As the night died down, things looked awesome, and great futures were on the horizon. A taxi pulled outside the school building. A man in a suit gazed across to the school, watching the students leave with a good smile on his face. He was only there for a second before his outline faded in the blank background.

Epilogue

And so, as all things naturally do, this is where our supernatural tale finally comes to a natural conclusion. There were no more battles to face nor anymore obstacles to overcome now. The strong values and morals had been played out and had won the day fair and square.

Families had been brought together, and people were united for their lives to be complete. Those who were lost in the mists of evil had found themselves once more.

Yet, despite the clarity being restored to the neighbourhood, there were still nerves as to what Molly, The Eyes and The Devil Student had done and had left in their wake. Many things had been taken from them, and the entities had made major impacts on their lives. Some wounds may never heal. Some sins cannot be forgiven.

Wesley Devon was at the shop corner. He was reading a newspaper. There was a small section covered on the myths and legends of the neighbourhood: Of course, there was nothing about The Eyes; Perhaps that story was better off being left in the dark. Hailey was just leaving the shop when she noticed her silent friend on his own. She gave him a silent wave as she rode away on her new bicycle.

Wesley's dad came out of the shop. He was carrying a crate of groceries with him. His son helped him load up the car. He noticed a bizarre concern on his son's face as he closed up the boot door.

'Are you ok, son?' He asked nervously. 'Whatever can the matter be, son?'

Devon sighed as he got into the passenger side. He wiped the sweat off his forehead. 'I guess I still feel sad about what went down between my sister and me. Do you reckon she is gone for good now?'

'Maybe…'

'Where do you think she'll go now?' The son asked now.

'Who can say?' The dad thought. 'Maybe she has found herself a way to move on to a much better place of existence for her. And maybe find herself some peace'.

'Suppose she remains as evils as she ever was in life?'

Peter nodded to this idea as he closed the driver's door and turned on the car.

'That is the strange thing there. All of us can wonder for the rest of our lives. But, we can never be sure. Maybe she will find a way back. Maybe she won't. Whatever the case, she'll still have you and your fearless friends to contend with. Who really knows these things? Only God really.

Now, let's go home for dinner'.

The car moved off from the curb and drove down the quiet road back to the Devon Household.

Mr. Devon was not wrong, though. They say that every misty, rainy night, or when the moon shines full in the sky at night, a creepy solitary image of a little girl can be seen walking through the world. And every year, on the date of her tragic accident, she haunts the neighbourhood: Walking scarily as a warning to others who misbehave, plunging her darkness into every gap; Shrieking like a lost soul.

FOREVER REFUSING TO LEAVE!